# TANK TALBOTT's GUIDE to GIRLS

Dori Hillestad Butler

Albert Whitman & Company
Morton Grove, Illinois

Library of Congress Cataloging-in-Publication Data

Butler, Dori Hillestad.
Tank Talbott's guide to girls / by Dori Hillestad Butler.
p. cm.
Summary: Having agreed to get math tutoring and to practice writing
over the summer to avoid flunking fifth grade, Tank learns some impor-
tant lessons about both family and fighting while writing a boy's guide
to understanding girls.
ISBN-13: 978-0-8075-7761-5 (hardcover)
ISBN-10: 0-8075-7761-8 (hardcover)
[1. Authorship—Fiction. 2. Conduct of life—Fiction. 3. Stepfamilies—
Fiction. 4. Schools—Fiction.]  I. Title. II. Series.
PZ7.B9759Tan 2006  [Fic]—dc22  2005026960

The diagram on page 23 and the handwritten portions
are by Andy Butler.
The cover art is by Barry Gott.

For more information about Albert Whitman & Company,
visit our web site at www.albertwhitman.com.

*For Andy, who inspires me.*

# Table of Contents

# 1
# The Big Meeting

I t had been sixty-two days since Tank Talbott's last fight, yet once again he found himself slouching against the hard wood bench outside the principal's office.

May as well get comfortable, he thought as he lay down on the bench and propped his feet up against the wall.

He'd been ordered to wait here while his mom, his stepdad, Dennis, his teacher, the principal, the school counselor, and the school social worker met in the conference room next door to the principal's office. Tank had never even met the school social worker before. It didn't seem right that people Tank didn't know got to decide what should happen to him while he himself was stuck out here on the bench.

"Feet off the wall, Mr. Talbott." Mrs. Grisham frowned at him over the top of her computer monitor. Mrs. Grisham was the school secretary. She always called people by their last names. Tank would've thought he'd spent enough time in here over the last six years to be on a first name basis with Mrs. Grisham. But then again, Tank happened to know that

Mrs. Grisham's first name was Pris. People named Pris probably weren't on a first-name basis with anyone.

"Mr. Talbott?" Mrs. Grisham said again. She gestured toward his feet.

With a heavy sigh, Tank plunked one foot down on the bench, then the other. Then he slowly raised himself up onto his elbow.

"Hey, Mrs. G.! Would it absolutely kill you to call me Tank?"

Mrs. Grisham adjusted her glasses. "If I were to call you anything other than Mr. Talbott, I would call you Thomas," she declared. Which only proved how much time Tank spent in this office. He could count on one hand the number of people who knew his first name was really Thomas.

"Okay, you can call me Mr. Talbott," Tank said quickly. "But you're the only one who can, Mrs. G. Doesn't that make you feel special?"

Mrs. Grisham gave Tank a long look, then went back to whatever she was doing on her computer.

Tank glanced up at the clock. 4:10. How long were these people going to talk, anyway? Tank's buddy Jason was probably waiting for him outside. Tank had told Jason not to wait. He didn't want Jason to know what was really going on in here, so he'd told him he had to talk to Mr. Burns about a school assignment (which wasn't exactly a lie) and that it might take a while. Unfortunately, Jason had said he didn't mind waiting.

Jason was probably sitting on the front steps of the school, hard at work on *The Dagmablob Returns,* his new movie script. *The Dagmablob Returns* was the sequel to *The Dagmablob,* Jason's first movie script.

Tank had no doubt in his mind *The Dagmablob* would one day be shown in theaters all across the country. And Tank would be partly responsible for that.

Tank was Jason's agent. His job was to: 1) find someone to produce Jason's movie script and 2) make sure Jason didn't get ripped off in the process. He and Jason would split everything fifty-fifty. Too bad some of those people in Hollywood didn't recognize a blockbuster when they saw one. Tank had sent Jason's script off to several real live movie producers and surprisingly enough, none of them had snapped it up. But neither Tank nor Jason was going to let a little rejection stop him. Tank kept sending the script out again as soon as it came back, and meanwhile, Jason had started a new script.

Tank hoped that Jason was so caught up in his new project right now that he didn't realize how long it was taking Tank to come out of school. The last thing he needed was for Jason to come looking for him.

Finally at 4:16, the door to Mrs. Meed's office swung open. "Okay, Tank," Mrs. Meed stuck her head out and smiled. *Why would she smile at a time like this?* "You can come in now."

"About time," Tank muttered as he dragged himself to his feet and followed Mrs. Meed inside her office.

Six very serious grown-ups were seated around a long, oval table. They all looked up when Tank walked into the room. Tank's mother had that I-don't-understand-what-I-did-wrong-with-this-boy look on her face. Dennis's look said just-wait-until-we-get-home-Mister! Tank wasn't afraid of Dennis. But he was a little bit afraid of his mom. And at the moment, he was very afraid of Mrs. Meed.

But Tank lifted his shoulders a couple times and tried to look cool. The key to success was: never let them see you sweat. Tank had read that somewhere. It may have even been in a book. These people could not say that Tank *never* read books.

"Sit down, Tank." Mrs. Meed gestured toward an open seat at the end of the table.

Tank sat. These people could not say that Tank never did what he was told, either.

"As you know, we're all concerned about your schoolwork," Mrs. Meed told Tank as she eased herself into the chair beside him. Tank kept his eyes glued to the ink dragon he'd started drawing on his jeans two days ago. It was a pretty good dragon, one of the best he'd ever drawn. It had realistic-looking scales, sharp teeth, and scary-looking eyes—

"Mr. Burns says there's a lot of work that you haven't turned in," Mrs. Meed went on. "And much of the work that you *have* turned in just isn't at the level that it should be."

Translation: We think you are lazy and stupid.

"I'm sure you know we've been talking about holding you back next year," Mrs. Meed said. "Having you repeat fifth grade. How do you feel about that?"

Tank raised his eyes enough to glare at Mrs. Meed and the other five people who were seated around the table. How did they think he felt about being held back? *I feel great about it. Just great.*

"Tank?" the counselor, Ms. Biggs, leaned forward as though she was trying to peer inside his brain. "How do you feel?"

Tank shrugged. What did it matter how he felt? They were going to do whatever they wanted no matter how he felt about it.

"It's clear from your Iowa Test of Basic Skills that you need some outside help with your math," Mrs. Meed said. "And don't worry, we're going to get you the help you need."

Tank slouched down in his seat.

"But your reading seems to be improving. And Mr.

Burns says your writing is coming along, too."

Tank lifted an eyebrow. Mr. Burns said that?

"That's right," Mr. Burns agreed, "when you bother to do the assignments. You've got a lot of interesting ideas, Tank. A lot of potential. Your compare-and-contrast essay on the differences between boys and girls was most entertaining."

Now Mom raised an eyebrow.

What could Tank say? Writing about the differences between boys and girls was way more interesting than writing book reports, or directions for how to make a peanut-butter sandwich, or all those other stupid assignments Mr. Burns came up with. Tank knew he couldn't spell or do grammar very well, but it was nice to know Mr. Burns thought he had good ideas.

"I really don't want to see you repeat fifth grade, Tank," Mrs. Meed said.

Translation: I am old and having you at this school is bad for my heart.

"And I don't think it's necessary to hold you back," Mrs. Meed went on. "So, the six of us have come up with a plan to help prepare you for middle school. We've got a contract here that I will sign, Mr. Burns will sign, your parents will sign, and you will sign."

Mrs. Meed handed Tank a sheet of paper titled *Learning Contract for Tank Talbott*. "If you do everything that's in the contract—and I mean everything, Tank, then, you will be allowed to go on to middle school with the rest of your classmates. Is that clear?"

"What's in the contract?" Tank asked suspiciously.

"Well, if you'll take a look, you'll see that you'll be spending a couple hours a day with a math tutor this summer," Mrs. Meed said.

"A couple hours a day? Every day?" Tank cried. He looked at the paper.

Yup. That was what the contract said, all right:

1. *Tank will work one-on-one with a math tutor (to be provided by the school district) every day, Monday through Friday (time to be deter mined).*
2. *Tank will show up on time.*
3. *Tank will behave appropriately.*
4. *Tank will do all assignments.*
5. *Tank will show academic growth in the area of mathematics.*

"So, is that it?" Tank asked. "I get a math tutor and then I pass sixth grade?"

"At the end of the summer, your tutor will make a recommendation based on how you've done with the assignments and tests. This person will decide whether you're ready for sixth-grade math."

"Now if you'll turn the contract over, Tank, you'll

notice there is one more thing you need to do if you want to pass fifth grade," Mr. Burns said.

Tank turned the paper over:

6. *Tank will complete writing assignment.*

"What writing assignment?" Tank asked.

"My writing assignment," Mr. Burns said. He slid a blue spiral notebook across the table to Tank. "I want you to write in this book every day."

Tank opened the notebook. It was blank. "Write what? Boring stuff like 'what I learned on my summer vacation'?"

"Anything you want. The only requirement is that you fill every page in this notebook by the end of the summer."

"Every page!" Tank cried. There were at least eighty pages in that notebook. And only three months of summer vacation. That was like . . . *a whole page almost every day*. No way could Tank do that.

"We'll meet again at the end of the summer," Mrs. Meed said. "If the tutor thinks you're ready for sixth-grade math, and this notebook is full, you'll pass fifth grade. If those conditions are not met, then we'll see you back here this fall. It's as simple as that."

Tank groaned. A private math class every day? An entire notebook full of writing? Where was the *vacation* in "summer vacation?"

"Do you understand what's expected of you, Tank?" Mrs. Meed asked.

"Yes," Tank said in a low voice.

"Good. Then sign the contract."

Tank signed it. Then his mom signed it. Mr. Burns signed it. And even though there wasn't a line for her, Mrs. Meed signed it, too.

"You will not flunk fifth grade, Tank," Mom said as they all stood up to leave.

Tank wasn't so sure about that.

# 2
# Tank Talbott's Guide to Girls

**Y**up. Just as Tank suspected, Jason was stretched out on the front steps of the school. But even before Tank got outside, he could tell that Jason wasn't working on his movie script. And he wasn't alone. That Mistress of Evil, Kelly Sears, and her trusty sidekick, Brandi Worth, were buzzing around Jason like a couple of flies.

What was it about Jason that attracted insects like Kelly and Brandi? Jason wasn't any uglier than Tank. In fact, Tank and Jason looked sort of alike. They were both tall and husky, both had dark hair and dark eyes. But Jason wore glasses. Tank didn't.

Why did Jason put up with Kelly and Brandi? They were *evil*. They always chased Tank and Jason during recess, and they got other girls to chase them, too. They tried to make Tank and Jason their slaves. Sometimes they even made prank phone calls to Tank or Jason from pay phones (Tank always knew it was them). Tank tried to get Jason to understand he didn't have to be nice to them, but Jason was the kind of guy who couldn't help being nice to everyone.

"Let's go, Tank," his stepdad said, giving Tank a little nudge. "I need to get back to work."

Tank didn't know why Dennis took time off work to come to this meeting, anyway. His mom could've handled it. But Dennis always went to everything that Mom went to.

Tank pushed open the door and strode out the building ahead of his parents.

Ew! Tank fanned the air in front of his nose as a cloud of perfume wafted over. Why did girls always smell like they took a bath in perfume?

"Don't be rude, Tank," Mom said under her breath. Then she smiled at Jason and those evil girls. "Hello, Jason. Girls."

Three heads swiveled around and glanced up at them. "Hey, Tank. Hey, Mr. and Mrs. Conway," Jason said, closing the notebook on his lap.

Jason hadn't let those girls read the script, had he? Tank wondered. It was *their* script. His and Jason's.

"What are you doing here so late, Tank?" The Mistress of Evil eyed him up and down. "Are those your parents?" She cocked her head. "Are you in trouble again?"

"No!" Tank said right away, hoping his folks wouldn't mention what they were doing here at school.

"Then why are your parents here?" Brandi asked.

"None of your business!" Tank said. "Hey, Mom, can I walk home with Jason? Just Jason," he said with a pointed look at the girls.

"I don't think so, Tank," Mom said. "We have things to do tonight."

Translation: We are not finished discussing this meeting.

"But we can give Jason a ride home if he'd like one," Mom offered.

"Sure," Jason said. He grabbed his notebook. "See you." He waved to the girls.

Dennis unlocked the van, and Tank and Jason crawled all the way to the back bench and plopped down. "What were you doing with the Mistress of Evil and her sidekick?" Tank asked.

"We were just talking. Kelly said—"

Who cared what Kelly said? "Jason, they're *girls*," Tank interrupted. "We don't talk to girls."

Jason laughed. "What do you mean we don't talk to girls? Girls are people, too, you know."

Tank snorted. He did not know any girls who were people. Except maybe his mom. And that depended on the day.

"How about you?" Jason asked, changing the subject. "What kind of meeting were you having with Mr. Burns? Why were your parents there?"

It was going to be harder to dodge that question with Jason than it had been with those girls. "I was just setting up an extra-credit project for over the summer." *Never let them see you sweat.*

"Extra credit? You?"

Tank glared at Jason. Just because they were friends now did not mean that Tank couldn't smack Jason if he had to. "Yeah, me. Why not?"

"Okay," Jason said. "So, what exactly is this extra-credit project?"

"Nothing."

"Come on. Tell me."

"It's . . . a writing thing."

Jason perked up. "What kind of writing thing?"

"A book." That sounded good. And it wasn't a lie. "I'm going to write a book over the summer."

"What kind of book?"

"I don't know yet."

"Well, that's great, Tank," Jason said. "If you're getting into writing, too, then you should come to the writing club at the library with me this summer."

"You have a writing club?" This was the first Tank had heard of it.

"Yeah. It's just for kids. And it's just starting up this summer. Kelly told me about it."

"Oh," Tank said. "I suppose that means the

Mistress of Evil is doing it, too?"

"She and Brandi are both doing it," Jason said. "That's what we were talking about when you came out."

By this time, they had reached Jason's house.

"Think about it," Jason said as he unbuckled his seat belt. "The group meets every Monday afternoon for six weeks. It'd be cool if we could go together."

It would be even cooler if the Mistress of Evil wasn't going to be there. "I'll think about it," Tank said.

**\* \* \***

"Any messages for me?" Tank asked when they got home.

"No," Mom replied.

"Any mail?" Tank asked. He should be hearing back from these Hollywood people any day now.

"No!" Mom said, as though Tank was just an ordinary fifth grader rather than a movie agent.

Mom pointed to a kitchen chair. "Sit, Tank."

Dennis came over and stood next to Mom. The two of them stood with their arms crossed like a couple of security guards.

Tank sat.

"Now, just so we understand each other," Mom began. "You are not going to fail fifth grade, Tank! It's not going to happen."

Had Mom been at the same meeting as Tank? Because it sounded to Tank as though flunking fifth grade could definitely happen.

Mom paced back and forth in front of Tank. "You're going to go to your math classes and you're going to do your assignments. Dennis will check them every night."

"That's right," Dennis piped up.

"You're going to write in that notebook every day," Mom continued. "And you're not going to even think about turning on the TV or the computer or going over to Jason's house until your schoolwork is done. Do you understand?"

Translation: You will have no life this summer. None whatsoever.

"Your mother's talking to you, Tank," Dennis said. "She deserves an answer."

"Yeah, yeah," Tank said. Hadn't he already said he'd do all that? Hadn't he signed a paper promising he'd do it? What else did they need? A signature in blood?

Boy, things sure were different around Tank's house now that Harry (Tank's last stepfather) was out of the picture and Dennis (Tank's new stepfather) was in the picture. Back when Mom was married to Harry, nobody cared much about Tank's schoolwork. Everyone was more concerned about avoiding Harry's temper.

But now that Mom had married Dennis, people expected things of Tank. They expected him to behave himself, not get into fights, do well in school . . . And if Tank didn't do what was expected of him, there were actual consequences.

"Good," Mom said. "Now, remember Dennis's girls are coming tomorrow—"

Tank tried not to groan in front of Dennis. Yeah, he knew those girls were coming, but he'd been trying to forget.

Anna, Mollie, and Gracie lived in Florida with their mom during the school year, but they spent summers with their dad. Tank's house was barely big enough for Mom, Dennis, Tank, and Tank's fourteen-year-old brother, Zack, the Human Destroyer. It certainly wasn't big enough for three obnoxious girls, too. But Mom and Dennis had been married two years now. And they still kissed and stuff, so it didn't look like they'd be getting divorced anytime soon. As long as Dennis was around, Dennis's kids would have to come every summer.

"You should be busy enough with your schoolwork this summer that you won't have time to be bothering them," Mom went on.

"Me? Bother them?" Tank cried. "What about them?

Who's going to stop them from bothering *me?*" Had nobody else noticed that the "bothering" went both ways last summer?

"We'll talk to them, too," Dennis said. "We'll make sure they understand that you have work to do every day."

"Wait a minute!" Tank cried. "I don't want them knowing I might flunk fifth grade!" He especially didn't want Mollie to know. Mollie was the worst of those girls. She was only five days older than Tank, but she always acted like she was so much better than him. If she knew about this, she would make Tank's entire summer unbearable.

"Do we have to tell them?" Tank asked. "Do we have to tell anyone?" After all, telling Zack would be almost as bad as telling Mollie.

Mom and Dennis glanced at each other.

"I haven't flunked yet," Tank pointed out. "And you keep saying I'm not going to flunk. So if I'm not going to flunk, why does anybody have to know I almost did?"

"I'm glad you're a little embarrassed about this, Tank," Mom said. "Maybe that'll motivate you to work harder this summer."

"I'll do whatever you want if you just keep this a secret. Please?" Tank dropped to his knees and pressed his hands together.

"All right, Tank," Dennis said finally. "For now, we'll

keep this between us."

"Thank you," Tank said, breathing a sigh of relief.

Dennis had just earned major points.

\* \* \*

A few minutes later, the back door slammed open and Zack stormed into the kitchen. He threw his backpack onto the kitchen table, then slammed his body into a chair. His long hair hung over his eyes. "I need a book," he said the way a guy on TV might say *I need a drink.*

"What kind of book?" Dennis asked.

"An instruction book," Zack said. "Something that explains what makes girls tick. Because us guys, we don't have a clue."

"I always said you don't have a clue," Tank said helpfully.

Zack ignored Tank. Which was very unusual for him. "If there was a book like that," Zack went on, "I'm telling you, it would be a bestseller. Whoever wrote it would be a millionaire."

Mom patted Zack's arm in sympathy. "What's the matter, honey?" she asked.

Zack looked down at the floor. "It's Dagmar," he said in a low voice. Dagmar was Jason's sister. She and Zack had been going out for the last couple of months.

"She dumped me," Zack said.

"Dagmar dumped you?" Tank laughed. "Ha! It's about time!"

"Tank," Mom and Dennis said together as Zack leaped to his feet, grabbed Tank by the shirt, and slammed him against the refrigerator door.

"I'll bet you had something to do with this, Thomas-the-Tank!" Zack said, twisting Tank's shirt in his fist. "You and your little worm friend."

"We did not!" Tank gasped beneath the weight of his brother.

"Boys!" Mom cried. "You know how I feel about fighting."

"I'm not fighting." Tank held his arms up in innocence as Dennis pulled Zack off of Tank.

Zack glared at Tank and Tank glared back. Then Tank smoothed out his shirt. "So why'd she dump you, anyway?" Tank asked. He couldn't wait to hear this.

"I don't know!" Zack yelled. "Why do girls do anything?"

When Zack said that, something clicked inside Tank's brain. *Book. Bestseller. Millionaire. Why do girls do anything?*

That was it! Tank could write his book on girls and why they do the things they do. There were a million things he could write about, things guys have been wondering since the beginning of time.

Mr. Burns said he could write anything he wanted; he just had to fill that whole notebook. If he was answering questions about why girls did the things they did, he could fill a notebook easy. He'd organize it so each page began with a question. And then he, Dr. Tank, would answer that question.

Tank looked at his brother with new respect. Who'd have thought a jerk like Zack would've given him such a great idea?

While Mom and Dennis sat down with Zack, Tank said, "I think I'll go start on some of those writing assignments."

"That's good, Tank," Mom said. "But remember, you need to get your things moved into Zack's room tonight. The girls will be here tomorrow afternoon."

"Can't they sleep in Lauren's room?" Tank's sister, Lauren, had just gotten married last month, so she didn't live at home anymore. Mom and Dennis had put a treadmill in her old room, but there was still plenty of room for three girls to sleep there, too. Especially if one slept on the treadmill. It didn't look *that* uncomfortable.

"Anna will sleep in Lauren's room," Mom said. "But Mollie and Gracie will need the bunk beds in your room again."

It was bad enough those girls had to come every

summer. It didn't seem right that Tank had to give up his room and move in with Zack the Destroyer, too. But on the bright side, Tank still had twenty-four hours to enjoy his room, so he decided to take advantage of it. He crawled up onto the top bunk (no doubt he'd be sleeping on the bottom bunk in Zack's room) and opened the blue notebook Mr. Burns had given him.

Page 1.

Hmm. If Tank was really going to write a book, then that book needed a cover. So on page 1, Tank wrote in big block letters: TANK TALBOTT'S GUIDE TO GIRLS. Then he turned to page 2.

A book about girls needed a diagram. So he drew a picture of a girl and then labeled all the parts. Well, all but the private parts. This was a school assignment, after all. Then he went on to write a little description about each of the parts he'd labeled. That way Mr. Burns couldn't say this page didn't count since it didn't have any writing.

Moving right along, Tank turned to page 3. He wrote: Why do girls do the things they do?

Writing a book was a piece of cake! At the rate he was going, he'd probably finish long before summer was over. Then maybe he could actually enjoy a little of his vacation.

\* \* \*

## Why do girls do the things they do?

Have you ever wondred why girls do the things they do? Why do they wear so much purfeume? Why do they paint their fingrnails? Why do they laugh like hieneas? And the ultimut question of the univers…how come when one has to go to the bathroom, they all have to go? Is there something inside a girl's brane that makes her do stuff a reguler person would never do?

Keep reading and I, Dr. Tank, will anser these questens and more. This book will not only give you an inside look at the female mind, it will also help you understand why they do the things they do. If you are a guy, it will help you servive! Garanteed!

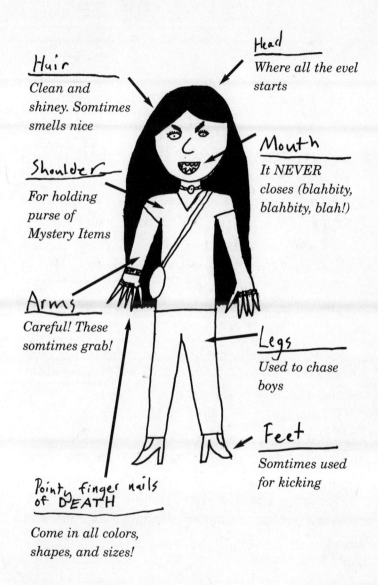

**Hair**
Clean and shiney. Somtimes smells nice

**Head**
Where all the evel starts

**Shoulder**
For holding purse of Mystery Items

**Mouth**
It NEVER closes (blahbity, blahbity, blah!)

**Arms**
Careful! These somtimes grab!

**Legs**
Used to chase boys

**Feet**
Somtimes used for kicking

**Pointy finger nails of DEATH**
Come in all colors, shapes, and sizes!

23

## 3
# Invasion of the Girls

**H**ow'd you do on your report card, Tank?" Jason asked when the two of them walked home from school the next day.

Tank tightened his grip on his backpack. "How'd you do on yours?" he countered.

"Okay, I guess." Jason held his report card in his hand. He opened it so Tank could see. Jason had gotten an "Excellent" in art, spelling, and conduct, and a "Satisfactory" in everything else. Tank would expect nothing less from Jason.

"Let me see yours," Jason said.

"I've got a lot of stuff in my backpack," Tank said, shifting his backpack. "It's too hard to get out." Like Jason, Tank had gotten an "Excellent" in art and a satisfactory in social studies, science, music, and P.E. Everything else, including conduct, was marked "Incomplete" for now. But Jason didn't need to know that.

"How's your new movie script coming?" Tank asked. You could always distract Jason by asking about his script.

Jason let out a big breath of air. "Not so good," he said. "Now that my sister and your brother broke up, I don't know what to write."

What a pitiful excuse for writer's block. "Your movie script isn't about them," Tank pointed out. "It's about a two-headed beast called the Dagmablob and her alien robot boyfriend, the Destroyer. And it's not a love story—"

"Well, it kind of is," Jason admitted.

Tank stopped walking. "You're writing a *love story?*" How was he supposed to sell a Hollywood producer on a love story?

Jason shrugged. "It's funny. I mean, a two-headed beast and an alien robot falling in love? Come on, Tank. Don't you think that's funny?"

"I don't know," Tank said warily. "I'd have to read it. Does it still have death and destruction and stuff?" *Please tell me you didn't take out all the good stuff.*

"Oh, yeah. It's just like the other movie," Jason said as they started walking again. "The Dagmablob bubbles up from the bottom of the city swimming pool and sucks up everything in her path, leaving the city in ruins. Then this alien robot beams down and they fall in love, which is really funny because the robot doesn't know how to kiss and the Dagmablob doesn't have a mouth for kissing—"

"Oh, man!" Tank slapped his hand to his head. "You have *kissing* in this movie, too?"

"Just a little. Anyway, they're so busy being in love that the townspeople don't know whether they're safe or not. But then they break up.

"At first I thought the Dagmablob could sort of go on this killing spree, but I just couldn't bring myself to write it. Not with the real Dagmar acting all depressed because she and Zack broke up. It just seemed . . . wrong."

"She's a blob," Tank said. "She's not your sister. She just happens to have a name that's sort of like your sister's name. I think having her go on a killing spree is a good idea. Especially if she just broke up with this robot. She's upset, right? So why wouldn't she go on a killing spree? Besides, people go to a horror movie to see killing. Not kissing."

"I know," Jason said. "But I'm thinking about trying to get the Dagmablob and the alien robot back together, too. Those kissing scenes were really funny. Maybe I'll bring it to that writing club at the library on Monday and see what people think of it there. Are you going, too?"

"Maybe," Tank said. "If I get more done on my book."

"More?" Jason's eyes widened. "You mean you've already started it?"

"Yup."

"That's great, Tank! What's it about?"

"Girls."

Jason's nose wrinkled. "But you don't like girls. Why would you want to write a book about them?"

"It's not that kind of book. I mean, it's a book for boys. It's like an instruction book. To help boys understand girls."

"Oh." Jason grinned. "Can I see it?"

"Well, I've only got a page, and it's probably not very good—"

"That's okay," Jason said right away. "I still want to see it. Please?"

"Well . . . "Tank liked that Jason wanted to see it. And Jason was the kind of guy who'd say all the right things, like: "This is really good, Tank." Even if it wasn't. That was one of the cool things about Jason.

So Tank unzipped his backpack, dug out his blue notebook, and handed it to Jason.

Jason opened to the first page.

Tank held his breath. What if Jason *didn't* tell him it was good? What if Jason thought it was stupid?

Tank knew there were probably a few words that weren't spelled right. Maybe Tank shouldn't have showed it to him yet—

Jason burst out laughing. "This is good, Tank!"

"Really?"

"Oh yeah." Jason handed the book back to Tank. "Is the whole thing going to be like this?"

"Yup," Tank said as he stuffed the notebook back into his backpack. "Each chapter will be a question you've always wanted to know about girls. So, if there's something you want to know, just ask. I'll try and work it in."

"You actually know the answers to all these questions?" Jason asked.

"Sure." Tank had a mom and a grandma, two aunts, a sister, and three stepsisters . . . plus he went to school with girls. He knew enough. What he didn't know he could always make up.

They stopped at the corner of Elm Street and Second Avenue, which was where they would go their separate ways.

"So, you're writing this book for extra credit?" Jason asked.

"Yup." Sort of.

"But why is Mr. Burns giving you extra credit when you're not even going to be at that school anymore?" Jason wondered.

That was a good question . . . a really good question. Too bad Tank didn't have a good answer . . .

"Will the extra credit follow you to middle school?" Jason asked.

"Yeah, that's it," Tank said. "Mr. Burns is going to make sure the extra credit gets counted at the middle school." Whew! Good save.

"Gee, I wonder if I could get extra credit for writing a movie script over the summer," Jason said.

"Probably not," Tank replied. "I think you had to set it up before school got out."

"Oh well." Jason shrugged. "I'd work on my movie script whether I got extra credit for it or not."

* * *

When Tank got home, he saw that Dennis's car was in the driveway. Which meant Dennis was back from the airport. Which meant Tank's house was now infested with girls.

"Be afraid," Tank said in a low voice as he put his hand on the doorknob. "Be very afraid." He slowly pushed open the door. Was it safe to go in? Tank couldn't tell.

He heard talking and giggling coming from the kitchen. Lots of giggling. And there was a pile of suitcases in the middle of the living room. Two, four, six, eight, ten suitcases? For three girls? That was more than three suitcases per girl! (Ha! And people said Tank needed help with math!)

"Tank?" Mom poked her head into the living room from the kitchen. "I thought I heard you come in. Come say hello to the girls." She motioned for him to hurry up about it.

Tank didn't know what the big rush was. He had all summer to say hello to them. But he followed his mom anyway.

"Greetings, Girls!" he said, saluting them. "Welcome to our humble home."

Whoa! Anna, Mollie, and Gracie all looked so different from last year. Anna's hair was longer, blonder, and straighter. She stood over by the sliding glass door, a cell phone attached to her ear. She didn't even notice Tank. Which wasn't unusual. Anna was sixteen and into her own weird stuff. The only time she had bothered with Tank last year was to correct his grammar or to inform him that something he was doing was harming the environment.

But Mollie and Gracie both eyed him from the kitchen table. Each had a bowl of peanut butter ice cream sitting in front of her. Which was interesting. Mom never bought peanut butter crunch ice cream for Tank and Zack.

"Hi, Tank," Gracie wiggled her chair from side to side and grinned. Gracie was seven and a little bit on the chubby side. She used to have hair that hung all the way to her butt, but now it was chopped off at her ears. Tiny pink studs sparkled in her earlobes.

"Tank." Mollie nodded coolly at him as though she were declaring a truce just for today. Some truce. She had on a yellow T-shirt that said Boys Are Stupid across her . . . whoa! Talk about change. She had shrunk down in some places (not that she'd ever been chubby like Gracie), filled out in other places, and when she stood up to rinse her ice cream bowl, Tank noticed that she was now almost half-a-head taller than he was.

Tank quickly averted his eyes. "So, is there any more ice cream?" he asked his mom.

"In the freezer," Mom replied.

"Excuse me," Tank said, giving Mollie a wide berth as he went to the freezer.

"You're excused," Mollie replied.

Mom must have sensed the tension between them because all of a sudden she said, "I hope you'll all get along a little better this year than you did last year."

"I got along," Gracie said, still wiggling from side to side.

"Of course you did, honey," Mom said to Gracie. "I

was talking about Tank and Mollie." Mom glanced at Tank. As though the gerbil incident, the washing machine incident, and the broken window were *his* fault.

"Hey, I'll leave her alone if she leaves me alone," he promised.

"Likewise," Mollie said, flipping her hair over her shoulder.

Translation: I will get you, Tank. But nobody will ever know it was me.

That night, the whole family went out for pizza. Even Lauren and her husband, David, came along. It was a family tradition to go out for pizza the night Dennis's kids arrived.

It was no great shock that Anna, Mollie, and Gracie did most of the talking. That was all girls ever did anyway—talk, talk, talk. First they talked about their mom's new book (she was a romance author). Then they talked about the weather in Florida. Then Gracie told about her new gymnastics teacher, Mollie bragged about her straight-A report card, and Anna blabbed on and on about how bad "a meat-based diet" was for you.

"You guys are awfully quiet," Lauren said to Tank and Zack once Anna stopped yakking long enough to take a breath.

Who could get a word in edgewise? Tank wondered.

"Wasn't today the last day of school?" Lauren asked. "Did you get your report cards?"

Tank did not want to talk about his report card. And it was obvious Zack didn't want to talk about anything. He just sat like a lump at the end of the table picking at a slice of pepperoni pizza. Tank had never seen Zack look so pathetic.

Tank leaned across the table. "In case you're wondering what's wrong with Zack, he's got girl trouble," he said in a low voice.

"Shut up!" Zack slugged Tank.

"Well, you do," Tank said, rubbing his arm.

"Girl trouble?" Anna leaned forward with interest. "Maybe we can help?"

Zack pressed his head against his hand. "No one can help," he said. "It's just over."

"Ah, the perils of youth," Lauren said, resting her head on David's shoulder. David put his arm around her.

"Listen," Mom said. "We need to talk about how things are going to go this summer."

Tank figured this was going to be another version of the you-must-all-get-along-this-summer-or-else speech. But instead it turned out to be the Dennis-

and-I-are-working-every-day-and-we-don't-want-Gracie-left-home-alone speech.

"Anna, Zack, I know you both have plans to work at Dairy Bar," Dennis said. Dennis owned the Dairy Bar, so it wasn't like they were getting *real* jobs.

"That means much of the responsibility of watching Gracie is going to fall to the two of you," Mom told Tank and Mollie.

It was? "But Mom!" Tank argued. "You know I have that *thing* every morning."

"What thing?" Mollie asked.

"None of your business!" Tank said.

"Yes, I know," Mom said. "Anna can watch Gracie in the mornings, and you and Mollie can share the responsibility in the afternoons."

"Daddy, you said I could go to that writing club at the library," Mollie whined.

"What writing club at the library?" Tank asked. "Not the one me and Jason are going to?" Mollie couldn't go to that. She just couldn't.

"I think there is only one writing club at the library," Mom said. "And it seems to me, if you both want to go to it, the only solution is for you to bring Gracie along."

"What?" Tank and Mollie said at the same time.

No way was Tank showing up at the writing club

with a seven-year-old!

"I don't mind going to the writing club at the library," Gracie said with a shrug.

"Good. Then it's settled," Dennis said.

Just when Tank thought his summer couldn't possibly get any worse.

* * *

Why do girls smell like they take a bath in Perfeume?

*Becaus they DO take baths in purfeume! It's a prooven fact that boys smell bettr than girls. That's why they just need sope when they shower. But girls smell so bad that somtimes sop isn't enuff. So they take a bath in purfeume. Don't hold it against them. They can't help that they smell bad.*

* * *

Why do girls Need so many suitcases when they go somewhere and why can't they carry them themselfs?

*Becaus the more stuff a girl has, the mor imprtant she feels. They also like to boss people*

*around and make people carry their big, impor-
tant suitcases.*

*Girls also like boys to be strong. Carrying lots
of sutcases all over the place makes you strong.*

*Girls like boys who are strong and who will
carry their sutcases. Then they can brag to their
frends about how important they are and how
strong thar boyfrends are.*

# 4
# Getting Along

**B**ang! Bang! Bang! "Tank? Are you up?" Mom called first thing Monday morning. Tank opened one eye. Sunlight streamed through the blinds in front of Zack's desk. It was the first day of summer vacation. Of course Tank wasn't up.

"Come on, Tank." Mom banged on the door again. "It's seven-thirty. You need to get up."

The mattress on the bed above Tank sagged and squeaked as Zack bounced around a couple times. Tank wondered whether the bunk could collapse down onto him, killing him instantly. If it did, Mom would be sorry she woke him so early. Mrs. Meed would be sorry for making Tank go to summer school. And Zack would be sorry he wasn't nicer to his only brother.

"If I'm not back to sleep in about ten seconds, you're dead," Zack said in a groggy voice.

Translation: I was a big, dumb jerk to take the top bunk. I dare you to wake me up even more.

So Tank put his feet up against the mattress and kicked as hard as he could.

"Hey!" Zack yelled. He leaned over the rail and

grabbed for Tank's hair. But Tank bolted out of bed before Zack could get him.

"Ha ha!" Tank laughed.

Zack hit his hand against the side of his bed. "You are so dead," he said.

"I am so scared," Tank replied. He gathered up yesterday's shorts and shirt off the bedroom floor and hightailed it to the door. When he yanked the door open, he practically ran right into his mom, who was standing in the hallway all dressed for work.

"Good." She nodded. "You're up. You don't want to be late for—"

"Mom! Shh!" Tank hissed. He cocked his head toward his closed bedroom door across the hall. He did not want those girls knowing where he was going.

"Oh, Tank," Mom said. "They didn't hear me. They're sound asleep."

"Don't bet on it," Tank muttered. Mollie probably never slept. She probably sat up all night thinking of ways to torture Tank.

"We're leaving in ten minutes," Mom warned as she continued down the hall. "I expect you to be ready."

Tank went to the bathroom and got dressed, but he'd forgotten to grab a pair of socks, so he went back to Zack's room. But when he tried the door, he found it locked.

"Hey, Doofus!" Tank pounded on the door. "Let me in."

Silence.

Tank pounded harder. "I don't know why you locked the door," he yelled through the closed door. "It's not like you're going to be able to go back to sleep with me pounding out here."

More silence.

"I bet I can pound longer than you can ignore me." Tank could go on pounding forever.

Then Tank heard a door open behind him. The door to *his* room. He slowly turned around. Mollie stood leaning against the door jamb, her arms crossed, smirking at him. She had on a pair of denim shorts and a pink T-shirt that said GIRLS RULE.

Rule what? Tank wondered. The bathroom? The makeup counter?

"Aw . . . did Zack lock you out, Tank?" Mollie asked.

"So what if he did? What's it to you?"

"Nothing." Mollie eyed her pink fingernail. "But I know something you don't know."

"Yeah, well. I know lots of things you don't know," Tank said.

"Do you know how to get into a locked room without a key?"

Don't ask, Tank told himself. Don't give her the

satisfaction. But somehow his mouth opened and the words, "Do you?" fell out.

"Yes, but I'm not going to tell you," she said.

"Tank!" Mom cried, storming down the hall. "Are you bothering Mollie?"

"No! I—"

"We don't have time for this. Where are your socks?" Mom glanced at her watch. "We should have been in the car two minutes ago!"

"Zack locked me out. I can't get my socks."

With a heavy sigh, Mom knocked on Zack's door. "Zack?" she called. "Oh, never mind. I'm sure there's a pair of your socks in the dryer. You can get them out of there. Let's go!" Mom hurried down the hall.

"Where are you going so early, Tank?" Mollie asked as she trailed behind him and Tank's mom.

"I told you last night," Tank said. "None of your business."

"That's okay. You don't have to tell me if you don't want to. I bet Zack will tell me."

Mom continued on into the laundry room, but Tank stopped next to the kitchen table. "No, he won't," he told Mollie. "Because he doesn't know, either!"

Ha! One point for Tank.

Mollie folded her arms across her chest. "Then it must be someplace you don't want anyone to know about. Like . . . maybe a ballet class."

Tank snorted. "Wrong!" Actually, his mom had made him take dance lessons a few months ago. She wanted him to know how to dance for Lauren's wedding. Fortunately, that humiliation was over now.

"Sewing class?" Mollie tried again.

"No."

"Math for dummies?"

Tank could feel his face heating up. "Definitely not!"

"Here are your socks, Tank," Mom said, tossing them at him. "Put them on. Your shoes are by the door. You can grab a couple of oatmeal squares and a juice box from the pantry. Have a good day, Mollie. I'll see you later."

Tank hopped across the kitchen on one foot as he struggled to put the sock on his other foot.

"See you later, Tank," Mollie said sweetly.

Translation: I may booby-trap your house while you're gone.

On the drive over to the middle school, Mom said, "I don't know why you can't be nicer to Dennis's girls."

"Me?" Tank gaped at his mother. "What about *them?* Mollie started bugging me the second she got up!"

"Probably because you said or did something to bug her."

"I did not!" Man! Things were pretty bad if you couldn't even count on your own mom to take your side. But when Dennis's kids were here, Mom always took their side. Always.

"I just want you to understand that coming here isn't easy for the girls."

Tank glanced at his mom through the corner of his eye. "What do you mean?"

"Think about it from their perspective, Tank. Their dad has a whole new life out here. He's got a new house, new wife, new kids. The girls are still trying to figure out how they fit into all that."

Tank slouched a little lower in his seat. He, Zack, and Lauren hadn't seen their real dad since he left when Tank was three. And Tank hoped he'd never have to see Harry again. After everything Tank's family had been through with Harry, Tank couldn't feel a lot of sympathy for Anna, Mollie, and Gracie. They at least had two relatively decent parents, even if those parents didn't live together.

Mom rested her hand on Tank's knee. "I'm just saying it would be nice if you and Dennis's kids could get along."

Translation: Please don't make things hard for Dennis and me by fighting with his kids.

"I'll try," Tank said grudgingly.

* * *

Tank's math tutor turned out to be an old, bald guy who used to teach advanced algebra at the high school, but was now retired. His name was Mr. Grisham.

"Mr. Grisham?" Tank repeated as he sat down at the table across from the man. "Do you know the Mrs. Grisham who works in the office at Central?"

Mr. Grisham smiled. "She's my wife."

"Oh," Tank said, surprised. He was dying to know whether Mr. Grisham called his wife Mrs. Grisham or whether he got to call her Pris. But since Mr. Grisham got to decide whether Tank passed fifth-grade math, Tank decided not to ask.

Mr. Grisham cleared his throat. "Shall we get started?" He opened Tank's math book to the first page.

Tank groaned. "We're going all the way back to the beginning of the book?"

"I thought we'd start at the beginning and see what you know," Mr. Grisham explained. "When it's clear you've mastered one concept, we'll move on to the next."

How would they ever get through the whole book at that rate? Tank wondered. What if they didn't get through the whole book? Could he pass fifth grade without getting through the whole fifth-grade math book?

But Mr. Grisham was the boss. So for the next hour and a half, Tank worked with Mr. Grisham on place value. It took forever to do just one problem because Mr. Grisham had to explain everything step by step. They only got through three pages before it was time to quit.

"I'd like you to do the problems from the practice test at the end of chapter one for homework tonight," Mr. Grisham told Tank.

Tank didn't realize he'd have math homework on top of all the time he spent getting tutored in math every day. He was going to be eating, sleeping, and breathing math all summer. And he still could flunk.

"What do you think, Mr. G.?" Tank asked as he gathered his stuff together. "Do I have any hope of passing fifth grade?"

"There's always hope, Tank. Don't ever let anyone tell you any different."

After class, Tank stepped outside into what felt like an oven. Man, was it hot! And since there was no one around to give Tank a ride, he had to walk home in the boiling-hot sun.

He considered stopping off at Jason's house on his way. Maybe Jason's mom would invite him to stay for lunch?

But when Tank turned onto Jason's street, he saw something very odd in Jason's driveway. A pink bike.

Jason did not own a pink bike. And as far as Tank

knew, neither did Jason's sister, Dagmar. In fact, Tank had been over at Jason's house once when Dagmar had announced that middle-school kids did not ride bikes.

So whose pink bike was that? Tank had to find out. Even though he was sweating like a dog, he took off running. He ran all the way to Jason's house, then skidded to a stop in the driveway.

Kelly Sears, the Mistress of Evil, was sitting beside Jason on his front porch. Jason's new movie script was lying open and forgotten beside him. He and the Mistress were actually smiling and talking to each other.

It was weird. There was no school project they could be working on. So what were they doing together?

"Tank!" Jason said suddenly when he noticed Tank standing there.

"What are you doing here?" Tank asked the Mistress at the exact same moment Jason asked him, "What are you doing here?"

Was it Tank's imagination or was the Mistress's face getting red? She glanced from Tank to Jason, then jumped to her feet. "Actually, I was just leaving," she said as she clomped down the wooden steps.

"Hey, don't leave on my account," Tank said. Though that was exactly what he wanted her to do.

The Mistress ignored him. She got on her bike, glanced over at Tank and Jason, then rode away.

Good riddance, Tank thought. He took the steps two at a time, then plopped down next to Jason.

"Hey." Tank nudged his buddy, who suddenly seemed unusually quiet. "What was she doing here?"

"Who?" Jason asked blankly.

"Duh! The Mistress of Evil." Tank pointed at her riding down the street.

"Oh. I don't know," Jason said, picking up his script. "She just uh, noticed me sitting out here and wanted to know what time the writing club starts this afternoon."

"But . . . wasn't she the one who told you about the writing club in the first place?" Tank asked.

"Yeah. I guess so."

"So why was she asking you what time it starts?" Tank pressed.

Jason shrugged. "I don't know."

Apparently the Mistress wasn't very smart.

\*\*\*

Why do girls have such short memerys?

It's a known fact that girls branes are not as diveloped as boys branes. Girl branes are smaller than boy branes so they can't hold as much informashun. And a lot of the space in their branes is taken up by stupid stuff like hair and cloes and lip gloss. When your too buzy worrying about what you're going to ware, you can't remember importint stuff like what time the writing club at the libbary starts.

# 5
# The Writing Club

**Y**our mom said you were supposed to be home at 11:00," Anna informed Tank the second he walked in the back door. As usual, she had a cell phone wedged between her shoulder and her ear. She and Mollie and Gracie had bread, peanut butter, and bananas spread out on the kitchen table.

Tank hoisted his backpack up onto his shoulder and glanced over at the clock on the microwave. It was 11:20. "I guess she didn't know how long it would take me to walk home," he said. "Any messages for me?"

"Who would call you?" Mollie asked.

"A Hollywood movie producer."

Mollie laughed. "I'm sure."

"It'll happen one of these days," Tank said. "Jason and me are going to get discovered. We're going to move to Hollywood and I'll probably never see you again."

Anna finished her call, then closed her phone, popped it into her front jeans pocket, and turned to Tank. "Actually, your mom did allow time for you to walk home. She said you were done with whatever it was you were doing at 10:30 and that it would take you half an hour to walk home."

"So? What's your point?" Tank asked.

"My point is you obviously didn't come straight home once you finished with whatever it was you were doing—"

"What were you doing?" Mollie asked, stepping toward Tank.

"Yeah, Tank. What were you doing?" Gracie echoed.

"We won't tell that you were late if you tell us where you were all morning," Mollie said.

They had him surrounded. But Tank managed to break free and make a run for his bedroom. Unfortunately, when he got there and tried the door, he found it was still locked.

"Hey," Tank called, dragging his backpack by the strap. He headed back to the kitchen. "Did Zack already leave for work?"

"Yup," Anna said. "He left about an hour ago."

Great. How was Tank supposed to get into that room?

"And I'm leaving now, too," Anna said as she gathered up a bunch of junk and stuffed it into a little black purse. "So that means you guys are in charge of Gracie."

"Why can't I be in charge of myself?" Gracie asked in a pouty voice.

"What a great idea," Tank said. "All in favor of Gracie being in charge of herself, raise your hand." Tank stuck his hand in the air.

Gracie grinned at Tank and raised her hand, too.

Mollie grabbed Gracie's arm and pulled it down. "You're seven. You can't be in charge of yourself."

"Well, I don't like it when you're in charge of me," Gracie told Mollie.

"Would you rather have Tank in charge of you instead of me?" Mollie asked.

Gracie's eyes grew wide and she quickly shook her head.

Well, who cared? It wasn't like Tank wanted to be in charge of Gracie anyway.

"Play nice, kids," Anna said. "Dad and your mom won't be happy if they come home and find you've killed each other." Then, with a wave, she was gone.

As soon as Tank set his backpack down, Mollie made a grab for it. But luckily, Tank managed to get it before she did.

"If I got your backpack, I could tell where you were this morning, couldn't I?" Mollie asked with an evil smile.

It was true. Tank's math book was in the backpack. So was the blue notebook that contained his *Guide to Girls*.

"Yeah, but you're never going to get my backpack," Tank said.

"Don't bet on it," Mollie said, grabbing (and missing) the backpack again. "I've got quick reflexes."

"Mine are quicker," Tank said. He pulled his backpack up onto his chest and fastened it there rather than to his back. Then he reached for the bread, the peanut butter, and a knife. But it wasn't easy to make himself a sandwich with a backpack attached to his front. Especially with two giggly, grabby girls reaching for it nonstop.

It wasn't fair. Tank couldn't get away from them. And he couldn't smack them. What else was he supposed to do?

Then he realized there was someplace he could go to get away from them. Someplace that had a lock. The bathroom.

Tank grabbed his sandwich, the bag of chips, and a Coke, then bolted from the table and down the hall.

"Where are you going, Tank?" Mollie giggled. She and Gracie were right on his heels.

Tank flew into the bathroom, kicked the door closed with his foot, and hit the lock with his elbow. His heart was racing. But he was safe.

Bang! Bang! Bang! The girls pounded on the door.

Tank set his lunch on the side of the tub, then dropped his backpack on the floor.

"You can't eat in there, Tank," Mollie said.

We'll see about that, Tank thought.

"Come on, Tank. Open up."

"What if one of us has to use the bathroom?"

Tank turned on the little shower radio and cranked the volume up as loud as it would go. Then he stepped inside the tub, closed the curtain, and sat down to eat his lunch. Either the radio drowned those girls out or they eventually gave up and went away.

Tank stayed in the bathtub until it was time to walk over to the writing club. Then he turned the radio off and stepped out of the tub.

He put his ear to the door before opening it. He didn't hear anything. Maybe the coast was clear? He picked up his backpack, strapped it to his front again, then opened the door.

Two unhappy-looking girls stood waiting on the other side of the door. Gracie's legs were crossed, and she was bouncing up and down. As soon as Tank stepped out of the way, she darted into the bathroom and slammed the door.

Mollie stood with her arms crossed, glaring at Tank. "That was really rude," she said.

"I agree," Tank said, hugging his backpack to his chest. "But since my mom really wants us to get along, I will accept your apology."

"My apology?" Mollie yelled. "What about your apology? There's only one bathroom in this whole house, you know. And Gracie really needed to go."

"Then you guys shouldn't have chased me in there," Tank said.

"Where are you going?" Mollie called as Tank walked away.

"To the writing club. It starts in fifteen minutes."

"You can't go by yourself," Mollie said. "We're supposed to walk over to the library together."

Translation: I don't know how to get to the library.

Tank sighed. Mollie would probably blab to his mom about him getting back late this morning. If she blabbed that Tank didn't walk to the library with them, too, he would probably really be in trouble. Not that there was much more his mom could take away from him this summer. Food? Air?

"Fine," he said. "But hurry up. I don't want to be late."

"Neither do I," Mollie said. "But I have to go to the bathroom."

**\* \* \***

There was a sign in the library that read: Children Under 8 Cannot Be Left Unattended in the Library.

"Gracie's only seven," Mollie said.

"Shh!" Tank hissed. "We could pretend she's eight."

"We could," Mollie agreed. "She's big for her age."

"I don't want to pretend I'm eight," Gracie said out loud. "Pretending is lying."

"No, no, no," Tank said quickly. "Pretending is 'stretching the truth.' Besides, the library only made that rule because most seven-year-olds aren't mature enough to be in the library by themselves. You're mature enough."

"That's right." Mollie nodded.

Gracie looked doubtful. "I don't want to be mature. Not if I have to stay out here all by myself."

"Don't be a baby," Mollie said, nudging her toward the Children's Room. "We'll come get you when we're done."

That's harsh, Tank thought. But if Mollie wasn't going to worry about Gracie, why should he? So, they left Gracie standing in front of a huge doll house, then hustled over to Meeting Room B, which was where the writing club met. Fortunately they weren't late. The teacher hadn't arrived yet.

There were nine kids seated around a big conference table like the one in Mrs. Meed's office at school.
Jason and two boys Tank didn't know sat at one end.
Kelly Sears, Brandi Worth, and four other girls sat at
the other end. Kelly and Brandi were whispering to
each other, but nobody else in the room was talking at
all.

"Hey," Tank said, sliding into a chair next to Jason.

Jason glanced up from his script. "Hey," he said.

Mollie walked around the table and sat down next
to the Mistress of Evil.

"I like your shirt," the Mistress nodded at Mollie's
GIRLS RULE shirt.

"Thanks." Mollie grinned. It figured the two of
them would hit it off.

"Good afternoon everyone," came a voice behind
Tank.

A woman with long, light brown and grayish hair
walked in carrying a stack of books with titles like:
*Teaching Writing* and *How to Get Kids Excited about
Writing*. Her colorful skirt swished and her bracelets
jangled when she walked.

The woman set her stuff down in front of one of
the empty chairs between the boys and the girls and
smiled at everyone. "I'm Karen Sterling. I'm going to
be leading the writing club this summer. I'm so glad

to find kids who like writing so much that they want to do it during summer vacation. I hope you'll all bring stories you're working on and share them with the group each week."

One of the girls Tank didn't know raised her hand. "But I don't write stories. I write poetry."

"That's fine," Ms. Sterling said.

"Jason here doesn't write stories, either," Tank said, pointing his thumb at Jason. "He writes movie scripts. I'm his agent. That means I'm trying to find a producer who will make his movies."

"Really?" Ms. Sterling smiled. "How interesting."

"My mother is an author," Mollie spoke up. "She says having a bad agent is worse than having no agent."

"Good thing I'm not a bad agent," Tank said.

Ms. Sterling turned toward Mollie with interest. "Your mother is an author?"

So Mollie wasted ten minutes of their time bragging about her mom, the romance author, while Tank drummed his fingers against the table.

Finally, Ms. Sterling remembered she was supposed to be teaching a class here, so she stopped blabbing with Mollie and got down to business. First they went around the table and everyone said their names. Of course, the girls had to go first. Girls always go first.

There was Ashlyn (she was the one who wrote poetry), Katie, another Caity (only this one was spelled different), Alex, Kelly, Brandi, and Mollie. The boys were Travis, Ned, Jason, and Tank.

"Tank?" Ms. Sterling peered curiously at him. "Is that your real name?"

"Sure is. Tank Talbott. That's me." He slapped his chest with pride.

"It is not!" Mollie said. "His real name is Thomas. But everyone calls him Tank because he looks like one."

That wasn't exactly how Tank got his nickname, but if that was what Mollie thought, he didn't care. It was better than the truth—that it had come from a little kids' TV show about a blue train.

"You think you're so smart," he said.

"No, I *know* I'm smart," Mollie countered.

"Are you two related?" Ms. Sterling asked.

"No!" Tank and Mollie both answered right away.

"I just have to live with him for the summer because my dad married his mom," Mollie said. Which started the Mistress and Brandi whispering again.

"Yeah, but what's even worse is I have to live with her," Tank said.

"Hmm," Ms. Sterling said. "Have either of you ever considered writing about your family? I think it would be fun to hear about your family from two different perspectives." Then Ms. Sterling launched into a ten-minute lecture on how ideas are all around us and you just have to reach out and grab them.

"What's really interesting," Ms. Sterling went on, "is how two people can start with the same idea, but end up with totally different pieces of writing."

Translation: I'm not choosing sides here.

"Yes, you can end up with a good story, like mine would be," Mollie said cheerfully. "Or you can end up with a piece of . . . well, whatever Tank turns in."

The girls all laughed.

But Ms. Sterling wasn't amused. "I want you all to understand that there are to be no put-downs in this class. In particular there are to be no put-downs regarding someone's writing. Does everyone understand? I want you all to feel free to share whatever you're working on. We're here to help each other, not hurt each other."

Nobody was allowed to criticize? Ever? Well, in that case . . . Tank raised his hand.

"Yes, Tank," Ms. Sterling called on him.

"I'm working on a book that I'd like to share."

"Really?" Ms. Sterling swiveled her chair toward Tank. "What's it about?"

"Well, it's not a story book. It's an informational book." Tank reached into his backpack and pulled out his

# The Writing Club

notebook. "It's called *Tank Talbott's Guide to Girls.*"

"You're writing a book about girls?" The Mistress raised her eyebrow.

"Yup," Tank said. "And you heard what Ms. S. said. You can't criticize it."

"I'm sure if somebody has a helpful comment on how you might improve the piece, you wouldn't mind hearing it, would you, Tank?" Ms. Sterling asked.

Tank thought about it for a couple of seconds. "I guess that would be okay." After all, there were three other guys here who could probably give him some good ideas.

Before Tank started reading, Ms. Sterling said there were two rules: 1) Nobody talks while the writer is reading. And 2) when the writer is done reading, people first have to tell the reader something they like about what they heard. Then if someone has a suggestion for how to improve the work, they can suggest it.

"Those are good rules, Ms. S.," Tank said.

Ms. Sterling blinked. "Thank you, Tank." She sat back in her chair. "You can start reading any time."

So Tank opened up his notebook, cleared his throat, and read his introduction. The boys at his end of the table snickered. But the girls just stared at him like they didn't quite get it.

59

When he got to the end of the introduction, he turned the page and showed everyone his diagram of the girl. Travis, the boy who was sitting next to Tank, laughed out loud. Even Ms. Sterling smiled a little.

"We can't see that down here," Mollie complained.

"I'll show it to you when I finish reading," Tank said. He turned the page and read about why girls smell like they took a bath in perfume. Then he read why girls need so many suitcases and why girls have such short memories. The guys were loving it, Tank could tell. But the girls were pretty quiet.

When Tank got to the end, he set his notebook down. "That's all I have," he said.

"Darn," Travis said. "I want to hear more."

Tank grinned. That Travis guy was all right.

"Well, that was certainly interesting," Ms. Sterling said. "Very imaginative."

"What makes you think you're qualified to write a book about girls?" Mollie asked.

"Uh-uh-uh." Ms. Sterling shook her finger. "Positive comments first, Mollie."

"But this isn't really a comment," Mollie said. "It's a question. I just want to know his qualifications. Isn't that okay?"

"My qualifications are I'm a human being who has spent time around girls," Tank said, rifling the edges of his notebook. "Too much time around girls."

Travis snickered again.

The other boy, Ned, nodded. "I thought it was really funny," he said.

"Me, too," Travis said. "You should write more."

"Have we had enough positive comments yet?" the Mistress asked.

"Do you have a constructive comment to make, Kelly?" Ms. Sterling asked.

"Yes," the Mistress folded her hands politely in front of her. "I would like to suggest that Tank check his facts. Because some of them are wrong."

"All of them are wrong," Katie or Caity said.

"Oh, come on," Jason said. "Tank's just being funny. You shouldn't take this stuff so seriously."

"Yeah," Tank said. Girls could be so sensitive!

"Well, then maybe I should write something funny for next week," Mollie said.

"We all should," the Mistress put in as the other girls nodded.

"I think that's an excellent idea," Ms. Sterling said. "Why don't you all work on something funny for next week. Let's see who can make us laugh the hardest."

* * *

# Why do Girls Be so sensitave?

*Girls are very sensative. And they dont like jokes. So dont tell them any jokes. They wont laff. In fact if you tell a girl a joke she might cry. Do you know why? Its because she doesnt get your joke.*

*But gess what? If you get two or more girls together at one time, they will laff like crazy even though no ones telling any jokes. Its weerd. I think they do that becaus they dont want people to know they don't do jokes.*

\* \* \*

# Why do girls ALWAYS have to go first?

*Have you ever had a girl come up to you and say Lady's first? I bet you have becaus girls always have to go first. They are selfish and don't know how to wait there turns.*

*But do you know what? Its not a bad idea to let girls go first becaus gess what? If a girl is in front of you, that means shes not behind you. And if shes not behind you, she cant stab you in the back.*

# 6
# Problem Solving

**H**ey!" Tank called after Mollie as she scurried out of the conference room with the Mistress of Evil and those other girls. "We're supposed to walk together, remember?"

Brandi touched Mollie's arm. "I feel so sorry for you having to live with him," she said.

"Thanks," Mollie said appreciatively.

The Mistress of Evil pressed a scrap of paper into Mollie's hand. "Call me tomorrow. Maybe we can get together."

"No can do," Tank told the Mistress. "Mollie and I have to watch her little sister tomorrow. And the day after tomorrow. And the day after the day after tomorrow. And the day after—"

"I'll ask my dad if you can come to our house," Mollie interrupted.

What? No! That would mean the Mistress would come to Tank's house. She'd probably sit on Tank's bed, touch his things, breathe his air. They'd have to fumigate the whole house.

But then Tank remembered something. "Wait a minute," he said.

"What?" The Mistress of Evil put a hand on her hip.

"You can't have girls over," Tank informed Mollie. "My mom said no girls are allowed over when she and your dad are both gone." Those were Mom's exact words when she came home once and found Zack and Dagmar watching TV in the dark.

Mollie sniffed. "That rule is for you and Zack. Not me. It's so you don't make out with girls when no one is home. Not that any girl would ever want to make out with you."

And Mollie thought he would want to make out with some girl? "I don't know," he said. "I'd really hate for you to get in trouble for breaking the rule."

Mollie moved closer to the Mistress and whispered something in her ear. The Mistress glanced over at Tank and started giggling.

"I'll see you guys tomorrow," Mollie said, waving as the girls left.

Then Tank and Mollie headed back to the Children's Room in silence. They found Gracie slouched down in a beanbag chair with a Magic Tree House book. She glanced up at them as they drew closer.

"Did you have fun in here, Gracie?" Mollie asked.

"Well, it was fun until this boy came and started

bugging me," Gracie said in a small voice.

"What boy?" Tank asked, scanning the Children's Room. There were no other boys there besides him.

"He's not here anymore. The librarian made him leave."

"Why? What did he do?" Mollie asked.

"He kept taking stuff out of the dollhouse and not letting me have it. Then he called me a fat pig, and he followed me around making oinking noises. So the librarian made him leave."

"Well, if he bugs you again, just punch him," Tank suggested.

"Punch him?" Mollie looked at Tank like he was the alien from another planet instead of her. "That's your solution?"

"Sure." Tank shrugged. The kid probably thought Gracie was an easy target because she was fat. One punch would tell him otherwise.

"She'd get kicked out of the library," Mollie said.

"So go outside the library and punch him."

"Girls don't use fists to solve problems," Mollie said in a superior voice. "They use words instead of fists."

"Wrong," Tank said. "Girls actually create new problems when they open their mouths and use words. If that kid comes back, he's going to remember

Gracie got him kicked out. And if she's here when he is, he'll probably really let her have it."

Gracie's eyes widened in horror. But why lie to her? Tank knew what he was talking about. He himself had been known to pick on some poor slob once or twice. Especially if he knew he could get away with it. But the thing is, Tank never picked on anyone who was likely to fight back.

"Trust me," Tank said to Gracie as the three of them walked out of the library. "If you want the kid to leave you alone, punch him. He'll leave you alone. I guarantee it."

"Don't listen to him, Gracie," Mollie said. "He's just trying to get you in trouble!"

"I am not!" Tank argued. "I'm trying to help. But you don't want my help? Fine!" Tank stomped off ahead of them. What did he care if Gracie got picked on? She wasn't his problem.

When they got home, Zack was just locking the front door. He had on his old raggy jeans and the black T-shirt he always wore when his band practiced. A pair of drumsticks stuck out of his back jeans pocket.

"You off to band practice?" Tank asked as the girls went inside.

"No, I'm off to water aerobics," Zack replied.

"Gee, it's easy to see where I get my sense of humor," Tank said, leaning against the front door. "Is our room still locked?"

"It might be."

"Interesting. Because I was talking to Dagmar the other day and she said that was exactly why she dumped your sorry butt. Because you're so mean to your little brother."

Zack stopped walking. He turned around and walked back to Tank. "She told you that?"

"Maybe," Tank shrugged. In truth, he hadn't spoken to Dagmar since she and Zack broke up. He hadn't even seen her. But Tank hadn't heard that that wasn't the reason she dumped Zack, so it certainly could have been.

Zack scowled. "You're lying!" He slugged Tank in the arm, then headed back down the driveway.

"Maybe I am, maybe I'm not," Tank called after him.

No response.

Tank went into the house and down to the bedroom he shared with Zack. He tried the door. It was still locked.

Great, he thought as his backpack slipped from his shoulder. Just great.

* * *

"I brought my cribbage board along." Mollie hovered around her dad that night while he and Tank's mom cleaned up the dinner dishes. Tank was curled up in a living room chair, working on his *Guide to Girls.*

"Do you remember where I got it?" Mollie pressed.

Dennis glanced over at the wooden game board in Mollie's hand as he loaded glasses into the dishwasher. "Of course. We bought it at that Renaissance Fair a few years ago."

"That's right. Do you think we could play a game?" Mollie asked hopefully.

"Well," Dennis said, glancing over at Tank. "I need to talk to Tank for a little bit first."

Mollie's eyes narrowed. "What do you need to talk to him about?"

Tank knew exactly what Dennis wanted to talk to Tank about. Math. Dennis had promised to look over Tank's math every night. And Dennis was the kind of guy who kept his promises.

At least Dennis didn't tell Mollie what he and Tank were doing. He just said, "That's between me and Tank, honey."

Mollie's shoulders slumped.

Dennis put his arm around Mollie. "We can play when Tank and I are done, though. Okay?"

Mollie nodded, but Tank could tell she was still disappointed.

"Come on, Tank." Dennis motioned for Tank to follow him. "Let's go down to the study."

So Tank closed his notebook, picked up his backpack, and followed Dennis. The look Mollie shot him as he walked past was enough to make dandelions curl up and die.

Tank made a face back at Mollie behind Dennis's back. After all, going over math problems with her dad wasn't anything to get excited about.

It didn't take Dennis long to go over Tank's homework. "Problems three, six, and seven are wrong," he said. "And you still need to do problems ten through fifteen." Then he sat there and watched while Tank worked them out.

"If you'd rather play cribbage than go over my math, I wouldn't mind," Tank said. Math was hard enough by itself. It was even harder with Dennis hanging over his shoulder.

"I appreciate the thought, Tank," Dennis said. "But first we're going to make sure you get your work done."

"But I'm not even your kid. What do you care whether I get my work done?"

Dennis actually looked a little hurt. "I care, Tank," he said. And Tank could tell that he really did.

So Tank struggled through the rest of his problems with Dennis watching his every step. Whenever Tank started to make a mistake, Dennis would scratch his chin and say, "Are you sure about that?"

Then Tank would rub his eraser over what he'd just written and try again. Finally, they got through problems ten through fifteen. And for the first time in Tank didn't know how long, he could say he'd actually done all his homework.

Dennis stood up. "Would you like to join Mollie and me for a game of cribbage?"

Tank considered it. He knew his presence would irritate Mollie and that was worth something. But in the end he decided to go work some more on his *Guide to Girls*.

\* \* \*

For the next few days, Tank went to math in the mornings, then came home to a houseful of giggly girls (including the Mistress of Evil!) and a locked bedroom door.

Why did Tank have to stay home every afternoon when there was absolutely no place for him to be? It wasn't fair. He couldn't be in his own room, couldn't be in the room he was supposed to be sharing with

Zack, couldn't be in Lauren's old room (that was Anna's room for the summer). And now Gracie had taken over the family room.

"You know, I had to give up my room for you guys this summer," Tank told Gracie as he stood in the doorway, swinging his backpack. "Can't you hang out in my room instead of out here?"

"Can't you hang out in Zack's room?" Gracie countered.

"Well, I would, but Zack keeps locking me out," Tank said as he plopped down at one end of the couch.

Gracie was curled up at the other end. She was watching the Cartoon Network, which was what Tank wanted to do, too. He just didn't want to do it with Gracie.

"Why don't you tell your mom?" Gracie asked.

Tell my mom? Tank almost laughed out loud. It would be just like a girl to suggest he solve his problems by running to his mom.

"Wouldn't do any good," Tank said. "My mom's at work. She can't make Zack do something when she's not even here. Besides, when she got home, Zack would act all innocent, like 'oh, was that door locked? I'm so sorry.' And then he'd just lock it again tomorrow."

"Anna and Mollie do stuff like that to me, too," Gracie said.

"Really?"

Gracie nodded. "It stinks being the youngest."

"Sure does," Tank agreed. It was weird to think he and Gracie actually had something in common.

On Thursday, Mom gave Tank time off for good behavior. She let him go over to Jason's house after math class. Even though Tank had his backpack, he brought along a sweatshirt to hide his math book in after class. Just in case Jason peeked inside Tank's backpack.

Tank and Jason exchanged notebooks almost right away. Jason read what Tank had written on his *Guide to Girls,* and Tank read what Jason had written on his movie script. It didn't take Tank very long.

"This is it?" Tank said, flipping the page back and forth in Jason's notebook. Jason had only written two pages in the last three days. Even Tank had written more than that.

"I'm having trouble with this script," Jason said glumly.

"Well, once we sell your first script, then you'll feel like working harder on this one," Tank said.

Jason bit his lip. "What if we never sell it?"

"We'll sell it," Tank said with confidence.

Writers! Always looking on the dark side. As Jason's agent, Tank was beginning to think that half of his job was keeping Jason motivated and working. The other half was keeping up with the paperwork.

And it was hard to do that when he didn't even have an office (or a bedroom) of his own.

"Hey, do you know how to break into a locked room without a key?" Tank asked.

"I've heard you can do it with a credit card, but I've never tried it," Jason said.

"Would a library card work?" Tank asked.

"I don't know."

"Let's try it," Tank said. "Give me your library card. Then I'll go outside your room and you can lock your door and we'll see if I can get in."

"I don't know," Jason said nervously. "What if you wreck my library card?"

"I won't wreck it," Tank said. "Just go get it."

So Jason opened his top bureau drawer, pulled out his wallet, dug out his library card and handed it to Tank.

Tank went out into the hallway and Jason closed and locked the door. "Okay, how do I do this?" Tank asked. He couldn't exactly stick the card in the lock. Only a tiny corner of the card would fit. So he tried wedging it into the space where the door hits the jamb. But that didn't work, either.

Jason opened the door and pointed to the latch that was sticking out of the side of the door. "I think you need to use the card to make this thing go in."

"Duh. How do I do that?" Tank asked. "You can't

even get to that part of the door from out here."

"Really? Let's see." Jason came out into the hall, pulling the door closed behind him. "Library card?" he said, holding out his hand.

Tank handed him the card. Then Jason stuck the card into the gap where the door and the jamb came together. It didn't work for him, either.

"Told you," Tank said.

"Hmm," Jason said. He turned the doorknob to go back in, but it didn't budge. "Uh-oh," he said.

"What? We're not locked out, are we?" Tank asked.

Jason looked sheepish.

"Do you have a key for your room?" Tank asked.

"Of course! It's . . . in my room."

"Great," Tank said. "So what do we do now?"

Jason shrugged.

The two of them were still standing there staring at Jason's locked door when Dagmar (the former love of Zack's life) came out of her room. It was ninety degrees outside, but she had on a black T-shirt and jeans. Her black hair was combed up into a high ponytail that was held together with a black barrette and a bunch of pins. Even her toenails were painted black.

"What are you guys doing?" she asked, her eyes darting from the boys to Jason's closed door and back again.

"We're sort of locked out," Jason explained.

Dagmar laughed. "You're locked out of your own room?"

"Well," Jason said, looking to Tank for help.

"Zack keeps locking me out of our room," Tank explained. A cloud passed across Dagmar's face when Tank mentioned his brother. "So Jason was trying to show me how to get in with a library card. Only it didn't quite work."

Dagmar sniffed. "I don't doubt it." Then she reached up and pulled one of the pins out of her hair. Several strands of hair fell around her neck.

She pulled the pin apart. Then she walked over to Jason's door, stuck the pin inside the little hole in the middle of the doorknob, wiggled it around . . . and voila! The door popped open.

"Hey, how'd you do that?" Tank stared at the doorknob.

Dagmar just smiled mysteriously. She handed Tank the pin. "See if you can figure it out."

"Okay," Tank said, eager to try it out for himself.

So with the door standing open, Jason pushed the lock in on the back doorknob and Tank jimmied the pin inside the hole. The lock popped almost right away.

"I did it!" Tank let out a short laugh. "I really did it!"

"Very good," Dagmar said coolly. But she didn't make any move to leave. She just leaned against the wall and watched them.

"So, Tank," Dagmar said as she casually twisted a loose strand of hair around her finger. "I haven't seen you around in a while. How have you been?"

Dagmar Pfeiffer cares how I've been? Tank wondered. "Um . . . okay," he said carefully. Then, because he was actually more polite than most people gave him credit for, he said, "How have you been?"

"Okay," Dagmar replied. "How's . . . Zack?"

Ah. So that was what she really wanted to know.

"Is he . . . okay?" Dagmar asked.

Translation: Does he have another girlfriend yet?

"He's . . . " Tank wasn't sure what to say. He's a moron. He's a jerk. He's probably never going to get another girlfriend. But Tank settled on, "He's okay, too."

"Does he ever . . . " Dagmar stopped suddenly.

"Does he ever what?" Tank asked.

Dagmar took a breath, then started again. "When you're around him, do you worry—" She stopped again.

"Do I worry about what?"

Dagmar shook her head sadly. "Nothing. Never mind." She turned on her heels and walked away.

Tank and Jason looked at each other and shrugged. Neither one had any idea what that was about.

* * *

why do girls mop around like its the *END OF THE WORLD* if they lose Their boyfrends?

Simple. Becuz it has. What is a girl without a boy? Nothing!

# 7
# Mollie Strikes Back

Tank checked the mailbox when he got home. There was a thick brown envelope in the box. It was his self-addressed stamped envelope! He and Jason had heard back from another Hollywood producer.

Tank stuffed the rest of the mail back in the box and ripped the envelope open right there on the grass. Inside was Jason's spiral notebook. There wasn't even a letter this time. Just a little yellow post-it note that someone had written "Sorry, no" on and stuck to Jason's notebook.

Another rejection.

This was the fifth producer who had told them no! Tank could hardly believe it. Did all that sunshine in California turn people's brains to mush? Why weren't these people begging to turn Jason's script into a real movie?

Well, Tank had a book that listed addresses of Hollywood producers. He'd just find another producer and get Jason's movie script back in the mail again.

Tank went into the house. He could hear girl sounds coming from his room. Giggles and snorts.

Great. The Mistress of Evil was over. *Again.*

No matter. Tank had work to do.

As usual, the door to his and Zack's room was locked. But this time, Tank was going in. He reached into his front pocket and pulled out the hairpin that Jason's sister had given him. He stuck the pin inside the lock, wiggled it around a little . . . and like magic, the door popped open!

"Yes!" Tank raised his fist in victory.

Zack was lying on Tank's bed watching TV. He bolted up. "How'd you get in here?"

Tank stuffed his pin back inside his pocket. "You can't keep me out of here anymore. Dagmar showed me how to get into locked rooms."

Zack hit the mute button on the TV and sat up. "You saw Dagmar today?"

"Yup."

"What did she say? Did she ask about me?"

Tank had never seen his brother look so pathetic.

"Get off my bed," Tank said.

Surprisingly enough, Zack did. "So, did she ask about me?" he asked as he pulled out his desk chair and straddled it backwards.

"Yeah, she did."

"Well? What did she say?"

Tank couldn't remember a time when Zack had

been so interested in anything he had to say. There ought to be a way to use this to his advantage. Except what he had to say really wasn't all that interesting.

"She just asked how you were and I said you were fine and that was it," Tank said.

Zack let out a heavy sigh, then rested his chin on top of the chair. His hair fell over his eyes.

So, Tank wondered. If Zack was miserable without Dagmar, and Dagmar was miserable without Zack, why were they apart?

* * *

Tank was afraid to show Jason their latest rejection. Jason was having a hard enough time getting his second movie script written. But as Jason's agent, Tank knew he had to tell him.

So on the following Monday, Tank and Mollie dropped Gracie off in the Children's Room right before the writing club. Then Tank cornered Jason outside the conference room and broke the news.

"I figured," Jason said glumly. He headed in to the conference room and tossed his notebook onto the table.

"Now, don't get depressed," Tank said, following Jason. "I've already sent it out again. I sent it to a guy named Dan McCormick. I have a feeling Dan is our man."

"Maybe," Jason said. But he didn't sound too hopeful.

Tank and Jason sat quietly, waiting for class to start. But all the girls were yakking across the table. Why did girls have to talk ALL THE TIME?

Finally, they heard the jangly jewelry outside the room, and Ms. Sterling arrived.

"I started writing a book this week," Mollie announced the second Ms. Sterling stepped into the room.

"I read part of it," the Mistress said eagerly. She was sitting right next to Mollie. "It's really good. You've got to hear it, Ms. Sterling. You'll love it."

"Let the poor woman come in and sit down before you start hassling her," Tank said.

Girls! No consideration!

"That's okay, Tank," Ms. Sterling said as she set her pile of books down in front of the empty chair that divided the boys from the girls. "I'm sure we're all anxious to hear about Mollie's book, aren't we?" She glanced around the table.

A couple of the girls nodded. But Tank didn't hear any of the boys begging to hear about Mollie's book.

"What kind of book is it?" Ms. Sterling asked. She

pulled out her chair and sat down.

"Oh, it's a very important book," Mollie said, putting way too much emphasis on the word *important*. "One that no home, school, or library should be without."

Tank could just imagine.

"That sounds interesting," Ms. Sterling said. "Tell us more."

"Well, it's also going to be a long book," Mollie went on. "A very long book. In fact, I could probably spend my entire life writing this book and still not finish it."

Translation: This book will be the mother of all boring books.

"So, what's the book about?" Jason asked.

Tank winced. Lesson number one: when a girl starts talking, whatever you do, don't act interested!

Mollie smiled sweetly. "I'm glad you asked, Jason." She stood up. "Since there's such a great need for this book, I've put it on the Internet so people can read it while I'm working on it."

"You put your book on the Internet?" Tank repeated. He didn't even know you could do that.

"I sure did," Mollie bragged. Then she started making her way around the table, doling out colorful squares of paper to each person.

"What's this?" Travis asked, picking it up.

"Read it," Mollie said.

*"Mollie Conway's Guide to Boys?"* Ned read out loud.

"What?" Tank cried. "Let me see that!" He grabbed Ned's paper just as Mollie dropped another one in front of him.

The girls hadn't gotten their papers yet, so they all craned their necks to see the boys' papers. Well, Tank sure didn't need his paper (no way was he going to visit molliesguidetoboys.com). He slid it across the table to Alex or Ashlyn, whichever one had the long blond ponytail.

Alex-or-Ashlyn caught the paper and the girls on either side of her bunched closer to read it. They all put their hands in front of their mouths and giggled.

"Yeah, real funny," Tank said. "Mollie stole that idea from me!"

"You've written a guide to boys?" Mollie looked surprised.

"You know what I mean," Tank said.

"Aren't you the one who wanted to know about Tank's qualifications for writing a book about girls?" Travis asked. "What are your qualifications for writing a book about boys?"

Mollie sat back down across the table. "Same as

Tank's," she said. "I'm a human being who has spent time around boys."

"You're a copycat who has spent time around boys," Tank corrected.

"And . . ." Mollie slung an arm around the Mistress's shoulder. "My new best friend, Kelly Sears, knows a lot about psychology—"

"Psycho what?" Ned wrinkled his nose.

"PSY-CHOL-O-GY," Mollie said in a loud and slow voice.

"It's the study of human behavior," the Mistress said.

"People who are into psychology study how people act and figure out why they do what they do," Mollie said.

"So Kelly's been helping me with my book."

The Mistress smiled evilly at Tank.

"Well, last week we heard about why girls do the things they do," Ms. Sterling said. "So I think it's only fair that we hear the other side this week. Will you read us part of your work, Mollie?"

"I'd be happy to." Mollie opened the pink binder in front of her and started to read. *Mollie Conway's Guide to Boys.* Chapter One. Genetics."

Mollie glanced up at the boys. "For those of you who don't know what genetics is, it's the study of heredity. Like if you have brown hair, it's because one or both of your parents has brown hair."

Tank snorted. She was such a show-off.

Mollie flipped her hair behind her shoulder and continued. "Introduction. Let's talk about genetics. Everyone has two chromosomes. If you're a girl you have two X chromosomes. If you're a boy, you have one X and one Y chromosome. DNA is stored on your chromosomes. DNA makes you what you are."

Tank was bored already.

"The X chromosome is bigger than the Y chromosome," Mollie droned on. "That means it can hold more DNA. Girls have more DNA than boys. So girls are better than boys. They're smarter, prettier and better behaved. It's because they have more DNA."

"What?" Tank bellowed. He didn't know anything about X and Y chromo-whatevers, but he knew about DNA. Girls didn't have more of it than boys! (Did they?)

Jason frowned. "You made all that up," he said.

"I did not," Mollie said indignantly. "We learned about genetics and DNA in our gifted and talented class."

Translation: Hello! I am gifted and talented!

"That's just the beginning," the Mistress of Evil said. "She's got a lot more. Read some more, Mollie."

"What else do you want me to read?" Mollie asked. She flipped some pages in her notebook. "I have chapters on why boys are so loud, why boys are so obsessed with sports, why boys are so dumb—"

"That sounds like a put-down!" Travis interrupted.

"And then, my personal favorite . . . " She paused dramatically and glanced at Tank again. "I also have a chapter on why boys think with their fists instead of their brains."

"Oh, that's a good one!" the Mistress exclaimed. "Read that one!"

Tank turned to Ms. Sterling. "I thought you said no put-downs. Are you going to let her read this stuff?"

"The stuff Mollie wrote is no worse than what you read last week," the Mistress said.

"I think the girls have a point, Tank," Ms. Sterling said carefully. "Mollie's just trying to have a little fun. She doesn't mean these things any more than you meant what you wrote last week."

Tank actually did mean what he wrote last week. His explanations of female behavior made as much sense as anything else.

"Go ahead, Mollie," Ms. Sterling said. "Read one more of your chapters, then we'll move on to somebody else."

So Mollie stood up, cleared her throat again and

started reading. "The Big Bang. There is a scientific theory called the big bang theory. It means a bunch of gases exploded and suddenly the universe was created. That's sort of what happens inside a boy's brain."

"What?" Travis asked, wrinkling his forehead.

Mollie turned the page in her notebook and kept reading. "When a boy is asked to think about something, it's just too much work. His brain sort of explodes. Then his other body parts have to take over. For example, his fists."

If that was true, Tank would've jumped up right then and used his fists on Mollie. But Tank had a huge amount of self-control. Which only proved that his brain didn't work anything like Mollie said.

"That's why a boy's first solution to any problem is to fight. He can't use his brain to solve problems the same way a girl can. A boy's brain just isn't powerful enough." Mollie closed her notebook and took a bow.

The girls clapped. The boys just sat there.

"That was stupid," Tank said.

"Uh-uh." Ms. Sterling shook her finger at Tank. "Positive comments first."

"That was positively stupid?" Tank tried again.

"I thought it was funny," the Mistress said.

"And very well written," Ashlyn added.

"Very well researched," Katie or Caity put in.

The girls went on and on for ten minutes about how wonderful Mollie's piece was. Tank wanted to read some more from his *Guide to Girls,* but Ms. Sterling said that they had to give everyone a chance to read once before anyone could share a second time.

So Brandi read a funny story about her little sister. And then Ned read a story about his dog.

Tank tried to get Jason to read his script, but Jason didn't want to. "It's not very good," Jason whispered to Tank. "I don't want to read it to anyone until it's good."

When time was up, Mollie said, "Check out my web site this week, everyone. I'll be adding to my book every day. In fact, if you have a question about boys that you want me to answer, you can post it in the forum and I'll add it to my book as soon as I can."

Oh, brother, Tank thought. He put his notebook into his backpack and zipped it up. "Do you know how to put up a web site?" he asked Jason.

Jason shook his head. "Do you?"

"No. But I think we better try and figure it out."

* * *

Why can't girls <u>EVER SHUT UP</u>!!!!?

Wherever you are right now, stop and lissen. Is somebody talking? It's probally a girl.

Wherever you are right now, stop and look. Do you see a girl? She's probally talking.

Girls can't stop talking. Its like there branes are wired right to there mouths. Whatever there thinking just goes right from their branes to there mouths. Thats because there branes have no storedge. So whatever there thinking just flies right out.

Girls have one more problum to. There mouths don't close all the way like boys mouths do. So if they don't talk, if they just sit there with there mouths open, bugs will fly into there mouths. And everyone knows girls hate bugs. So that's why girls talk all the time.

# 8
# Mollie's Guide to Boys

**W**hat did you think of my book, Tank?" Mollie asked later that afternoon. Tank was sacked out on the couch, trying to watch Cartoon Network, and Mollie was blocking the TV.

"I already told you what I think," Tank said. "I think it's stupid."

"No, you don't." Mollie smiled evilly.

"Yes, I do. Now, move!" Tank tried to see around her.

Mollie didn't budge. "I bet you've already been to my web site."

"Actually, I haven't."

"I bet you can't wait to see what I'm going to put up next."

"I couldn't care less what you put up next."

"I bet it's driving you crazy that I have a web site and you don't," Mollie said. "That I'm smart enough to make a web site and you're not."

"I couldn't care less about your web site," Tank said as he grabbed his pillow and whaled it at Mollie. It hit her on the side of the head, then dropped to the floor.

She smiled as she picked it up. "Sure, you don't," she said, walking away with Tank's pillow.

Tank did not have a chance to check out Mollie's web site. That's because someone was always home. Until Saturday.

On Saturday, Zack and Anna were both working. And Mom, Dennis, Mollie, and Gracie decided to go on a bike ride. Mom and Dennis tried to get Tank to come, too, but about the last thing Tank wanted to do was go on a bike ride with all of them.

So Tank stood in front of the living room window, watching until all four of them had disappeared around a corner. Once he was satisfied they were gone, he made a dash for the computer.

When everything was up and running, Tank opened up Internet Explorer and went to www.molliesguidetoboys.com. It wasn't a fancy site. There was a picture of a teenage boy flexing his muscles. He had a really dorky expression on his face. Everything else on the site was text and links.

The main page just said: Hi, I'm Mollie. Welcome to the web site for my book entitled *Mollie's Guide to Boys*. Then there were links for "About Mollie," "About Mollie's Book," "Mollie's Guide to Boys," and "Forum."

Tank clicked on "About Mollie" first. Yawn. It was just a boring biography of Mollie. She was born in

Tampa, Florida. She had two sisters. She liked science and computers. Yadda, yadda, yadda. Tank didn't even read it all.

He clicked on "About Mollie's Book" next. This page was all about how Mollie got the idea to write a book about boys. "Boys are interesting creatures," it said. "Nobody really understands them. But my book attempts to unravel some of the mysteries of boys. Click on 'Mollie's Guide to Boys' and prepare to be enlightened."

Tank snorted. What that page should have said was: "I stole this idea from my brilliant stepbrother, Tank Talbott. I think I'm funny, but I'm really not. Go web surf somewhere else."

It about killed him to do it, but Tank clicked on "Mollie's Guide to Boys." He had to see what Mollie had written and how she'd designed that page.

The page that came up was a list of links. The first link was "Introduction." The others were all questions: Why are boys so loud? Why are boys so smelly? Why are boys obsessed with sports? Why do boys think with their fists instead of their brains? Why are boys' brains so small? Why don't boys care about clothes? Why do boys like cars and things that go fast? Tank counted down the list of links with his finger. There were thirty-two of them in all.

Tank clicked on "Why do boys think with their fists instead of their brains." It was the same thing Mollie had read at the writing club.

When had Mollie had time to do all this? If Tank had come up with thirty-two chapters about girls, he'd probably have most of his notebook filled.

Then Tank scrolled to the bottom of the page. There was a note that read: "This book is not yet available in stores. But if you'd like to support the author, please send check or money order to Mollie Conway." And then it listed both her Florida address and her dad's Illinois address.

What? She actually expected people to pay her for this garbage?

There was only one more link to click on. The link that said "Forum." Tank clicked on Forum and a page with lots of messages came up.

At the top it said: "Be a part of Mollie's book. If you have a burning question about boys, please post it here. Mollie will answer all questions in the order they were received. Then she will add all the new questions to her book."

Tank could hardly believe his eyes. Tons of girls had posted questions. Or offered suggestions. (One girl said Mollie should add a "Stupid Things Boys Have Done" link to her web site.) A couple of people had just posted messages like "great site." And two had actually said they were sending Mollie a check today.

Where had all these people come from? How did they hear about Mollie's site? She couldn't have had it up more than a week. They were probably all girls from the writing club, each of them pretending to be somebody else. No way were these all real girls from all over the world.

Were they?

Tank had to get a web site of his own up and running. But how? He didn't know anything about setting up a web site.

Well, how hard could it be? Mollie had done it. And Mollie wasn't that much smarter than he was. The fact that she was in the gifted and talented program and Tank was in danger of flunking fifth grade didn't mean a thing. Tank could do this! He could set up a web page for himself. He just . . . needed a plan.

Tank drummed his fingers on the table in front of him and stared at the computer screen. Plan, plan, plan, he said to himself, hoping that a plan would miraculously appear inside his head.

Ah ha! He knew what to do! He was sitting here at the edge of the computer information highway. People said you could find anything online. Maybe there were directions for how to set up a web site?

Tank went to a search engine and typed in "how to make a web page."

Yes! There were 1,962 results. Now Tank was getting somewhere. He clicked on the first one, but it was kind of complicated and hard to understand. So he clicked on the next one. That one talked about software you could get to help you set up a web site. The third one talked about a language called HTML.

Tank's mind boggled. There had to be an easier way.

Was there anybody he knew (besides Mollie) who had a web site? Anybody he knew who was really into computers and could help him?

Maybe his sister, Lauren? She worked with computers. Tank usually zoned out whenever Lauren talked about her job, so he wasn't entirely sure what she did. But he was pretty sure it had something to do with computers.

Tank reached for the phone and punched in his sister's number.

"Hello?" Lauren answered the phone.

"Hey. It's me. Tank."

"Tank? Tank who?"

"What do you mean 'Tank who?' How many Tanks do you know?"

"Only one. He's my little brother. But he never calls me, so it couldn't be him."

Tank did not have time for this. Mom and Dennis and Mollie and Gracie could be back any second.

"Well, it is me. And I need your help. I want to set up a web site. Can you tell me how to do it?"

"You want to set up a web site?" Lauren repeated.

"Yes."

"What for?"

"Well, I'm writing a book. And I want to advertise it on my web site."

Lauren paused for a second. Then she burst out laughing.

"What?" Tank said, annoyed. "What's so funny?" Just because Lauren was grown up didn't mean she was so great. "Kids can have web sites, too, you know. Mollie's got one. It's kind of stupid, but she's got one. It's molliesguidetoboys.com. I want to have a web site called tanktalbottsguidetogirls.com and I want it to be better than Mollie's. Now, can you help me or not?"

Tank could hear typing in the background. "What are you doing?" he asked. "Are you even listening to me?"

"Yes, I'm listening. I just want to check out Mollie's web site."

Tank waited. He could tell right when Lauren

TANK TALBOTT'S GUIDE TO GIRLS

logged on to Mollie's web site because she started laughing again. In fact, she was laughing pretty hard.

"Oh, forget it," Tank said. This was a bad idea. What was he thinking going to another girl for help?

"No wait!" Lauren said. "Don't hang up. I want to finish looking at this."

So Tank waited.

And waited.

And waited.

At least Lauren had stopped laughing. But it was taking her forever to read through Mollie's site.

"Hmm," Lauren said finally.

"Hmm what?" Tank said.

"This is a really bad idea," Lauren said.

"What? Mollie's web site?" Tank asked. Lauren thought Mollie's web site was a bad idea?

"Do Mom and Dennis know about this?" Lauren asked.

"I don't know. Probably not." Mom and Dennis were in their own little world sometimes.

"Do they know she's got her name and address on there for the whole world to see? She's a kid. That's a really bad idea."

"Yes, it is," Tank said as though he knew it all along. Would Mollie's web site have to come down? Wouldn't *that* be a shame.

"And she's asking strangers to send her money?" Lauren cried. "Another really bad idea!"

"Well, it sounds like our Mollie has been a very bad girl," Tank said in his most mature voice, while inside he was thinking, Mollie's in trouble! Mollie's in trouble! He almost started doing the happy dance right then and there.

"Don't worry. I will let Mom and Dennis know about this as soon as they get back from their bike ride," Tank promised. Because, after all, there was a difference between tattling and telling people something they need to know.

"No," Lauren said. "I will tell them. Why don't you have Mom give me a call as soon as she gets home, okay?"

"Sure," Tank said. Even better to let Lauren do the telling.

* * *

As requested, Tank told Mom to call Lauren when she got home. The two of them talked for ten minutes while Tank and Gracie sat on the couch in the family room and watched TV.

When Mom hung up, she called Dennis into the family room. "Can you two please go someplace else?"

Mom asked Tank and Gracie. "Dennis and I need to talk about something."

"That sounds serious," Dennis said.

"It is serious," Mom said.

So Gracie turned off the TV, then headed down the hall to her room. Tank started to follow but then hung back to listen to what was going on in the family room.

"Mollie did what?" Dennis asked.

"Let's check it out," Mom said as she sat down at the computer. Dennis leaned over her shoulder. Their backs were to Tank, so he stood in the doorway watching. Listening.

Tank heard typing. Then clicking. Then a gasp. And about three seconds later, Tank had to leap out of the way because Dennis went storming out of the family room. Mom was right behind him. If they even noticed Tank standing there, they didn't say anything.

Tank hurried through the kitchen and stood watching in the living room as Dennis pounded on Tank's former bedroom door. Gracie opened the door.

"Gracie, we need to talk to Mollie. Can you please go someplace else?" Dennis asked.

"But I just was someplace else."

"Gracie," Dennis said in a warning voice.

"Okay, okay," Gracie said as she plodded down the hall. She stopped when she saw Tank. "What's going on?"

"Mollie's in trouble," Tank said. He couldn't stop the smile from spreading across his face.

"How come?"

"Shh," Tank said. "Let's listen."

The two of them tiptoed down the hall and tried to listen outside Tank's former room. But they could only hear bits and pieces of what was going on.

It was enough that Mollie was in trouble and Tank wasn't, Tank decided. So he went into his room across the hall, and Gracie went back to the family room.

Mom and Dennis talked to Mollie for a long time. When the door finally opened across the hall, Mom and Dennis left without saying a word.

Mollie wiped the back of her hand across her eyes (What? Was she crying?) as she got up off Tank's bottom bunk and came to close her door. But before she closed it, she noticed Tank. She narrowed her eyes.

"You better sleep with your eyes open, Tank," she said in a low voice. "Because I'll get you for this. Sometime when you least expect it, I'll get you!"

And with that, she slammed her door.

# 9
# Waiting and Wondering

**M**ollie was the one who had put her name and address on her web site. *She* was the one who had asked for money online. Yet, somehow she acted like it was all Tank's fault that her dad made her take her web site down. And one way or another, Tank knew she would make him pay.

Fortunately, Tank didn't actually see much of Mollie over the next few days. The two of them were supposed to be watching Gracie together in the afternoons, but most afternoons Gracie was sacked out on the couch in the family room watching TV. Mollie was in their room with the door closed, doing who knew what. Probably planning her revenge on Tank.

Mollie didn't really participate much in family stuff over the next few days, either. She came out of her room to eat, but she didn't talk to anyone during the meal. And as soon as she finished, she asked to be excused.

"Would you like to play some catch tonight?" Dennis asked Mollie as she pushed her chair back on Thursday night.

"No thanks," Mollie said coolly.

"Oh, come on," Dennis pressed. "I bet Tank would let you borrow his glove."

Not unless I absolutely have to, Tank thought. He wasn't playing baseball this year, but still. His glove was his glove. He didn't want other hands grubbing it up. Especially not Mollie's.

But Tank didn't need to worry. "I don't play catch anymore," Mollie said.

"What are you talking about?" Dennis asked. "You love to play catch."

"I did when I was five," Mollie grumped. "I'm eleven now. In case you hadn't noticed."

Translation: I'm a real crab now. In case you hadn't noticed.

On Monday afternoon, Tank, Mollie and Gracie walked over to the library. Walking in the heat was never fun, but this walk was even more uncomfortable because no one was saying anything.

*Sometime when you least expect it, I'll get you,* Mollie had said. Was today the day? Tank wondered.

"How come no one's saying anything?" Gracie asked after they'd gone two blocks.

Tank glanced at Mollie. Her jaw was tight, and her eyes were focused straight ahead. She didn't say a word.

Neither did Tank.

Why was it girls, who normally couldn't shut up, suddenly gave you the silent treatment when they were mad at you? Tank wondered. What was that about? When a guy gets mad, he tells you. Or he punches you. One way or the other, it's over in a matter of minutes. But a girl? A girl could hang onto a grudge forever. Even if it wasn't your fault.

"I'm not the one who made you take your web site down," Tank said finally.

Mollie didn't respond.

"I mean, it was pretty stupid putting your name and address on there." Tank couldn't help but rub it in a little. "And I can't believe you actually expected people to send you money. But whatever. The thing is, I'm not the one who made you take it down. So, I don't know what you're mad at me for."

Still no response.

"Is that why you're not talking?" Gracie asked Mollie. "Because you think Tank made you take your web site down?"

Silence.

"What was on your web site?" Gracie pressed.

"Oh, it was terrible," Tank said. "It had all kinds of illegal stuff—"

"It did not!" Mollie stopped walking.

Tank grinned. "Ha! Made you talk!"

Tank could practically see the steam bursting out of Mollie's ears. She started walking again. Walking fast.

"I thought girls used words to solve their problems," Tank said, chasing after her. "If you're so good with words, why aren't you talking to me?"

"If you're so smart, why don't you figure it out and put it in your stupid book?" Mollie said.

"If I could figure it out, I would put it in my book."

At the writing club, Mollie acted like there was nothing wrong. She sat with the girls and talked and giggled with them like normal. Nobody knew there was a war going on at the Conway house.

Several of the kids who had never read any of their work before read today. But when all of them had finished reading, there was still time left. So Ms. Sterling asked Tank if he'd like to share another page or two from his book.

Several of the girls groaned. Molly slumped back in her seat

"Sure!" Tank said as he flipped through his notebook. He had so many good pages, it was hard to decide which one to read.

"What would you guys like to hear?" he asked.

"Do you have one on why girls are so obsessed with clothes?" Travis asked. "My sister has so many clothes they don't even fit in her closet."

"Mine, too," Jason put in.

"I do have an answer for that," Tank said as he flipped the pages. "Here it is! 'Why Do Girls Need So Many Clothes? Girls need a lot of clothes. More than the average person. It's because girls have really bad germs. Their germs are so bad they can destroy clothing. That's why girls always need new clothes. If they didn't get new clothes, they would have nothing to wear. Because their other clothes would disintegrate after three wearings.'"

"That is so stupid," the Mistress of Evil said. "It's not even funny."

"What happened to 'good comments first'?" Tank asked Ms. Sterling.

But before she could answer, Mollie interrupted. "If I ever get my hands on that book of his, I'll rip it apart page by page."

"Why?" Tank asked. "Are you afraid to let people know the truth about girls? What else would you guys like to know about girls?" he asked the boys.

"Maybe we should move on to someone else," Ms. Sterling suggested. But everyone ignored her.

"I'd like to know why girls wear so much makeup," Jason said.

If looks could kill, Jason would be dead from the

look the Mistress was giving him.

"What?" Jason asked her.

But the Mistress just turned away.

"Is there anybody else—" Ms. Sterling began.

"I'd like to know why girls wear that sparkly makeup on their faces," Ned interrupted. "What's that about?"

"Oh, I don't have that one in my book yet," Tank said. "But it's a good one."

Ms. Sterling rubbed her temples like she was getting a headache.

"I'd like to know why girls are so afraid of spiders," Travis said.

"I never wrote about that, either," Tank said, turning to a fresh page. At least he was getting ideas for new subjects to write about.

"Okay, this is starting to get a little out of hand," Ms. Sterling said, her voice rising above everyone else's. "I think we've discussed Tank's project enough for one day. Is there anybody else who'd like to share?"

Mollie raised her hand. "I would."

Ms. Sterling didn't exactly look pleased to see Mollie's hand. But Mollie's was the only hand that was up.

"Are you still working on the same project you brought last week?" Ms. Sterling asked.

"Yes. Unfortunately, I was forced to take my web site down," Mollie said with a pointed look at Tank. "But that little setback has only made me more determined to finish my book so I can get it published. My mom's agent is already interested."

"Wow, really? It's going to be a real book? Are you going to get lots of money?" The girls all started talking at once.

Tank accidentally pushed down on his pencil and broke the lead.

"Y-you've actually spoken with a literary agent?" Ms. Sterling asked.

"I talk to my mom's agent all the time," Mollie said, like it was no big deal.

Tank felt his insides twist around in jealousy. He and Jason had been trying to sell Jason's movie script for months. Yet, Mollie could call up her mom's literary agent a week and a half after starting her book, which she was only writing to annoy Tank, and now she was actually going to get it published? Just like that? It wasn't fair!

Mollie had indeed found a way to get her revenge on Tank. And it was a bitter, bitter revenge.

"Should I read?" Mollie asked.

"Yes, go ahead," Ms. Sterling said.

"'Why do boys always worm their way into things

that are none of their business?'" Mollie began.

"Hey, that's one of mine, too!" Tank said, turning pages. "I've got 'why do girls always stick their noses into stuff that's none of their beeswax?'"

Mollie ignored Tank and kept on reading. 'Boys always worm their way in where they don't belong. They do it because their own lives aren't very interesting. Girls are way more interesting than boys. They're way more creative than boys. And boys don't like that, so they butt in where they don't belong and screw everything up.'

"Oh, mine's different than that," Tank said. "Let me read mine—"

"Wait a minute," the Mistress spoke up. "We haven't discussed Mollie's piece yet."

"And you already read something today, Tank," Ashlyn said. "You don't get to read again."

"But this is short," Tank argued. "And it fits with Mollie's. 'Why do girls always butt into stuff that's none of their beeswax? It has to do with their noses. Girls noses are very big and long. They're like periscopes that work their way into other people's business—'"

"Okay, stop!" Ms. Sterling banged her hand on the table. "Just stop."

It was suddenly very quiet in the conference room.

Ms. Sterling glanced around the room at each person.

"When the two of you started this *Guide to Girls* and *Guide to Boys,* I thought you were both doing it in good, clean fun. But now I'm not so sure. It seems this project has degraded into something really negative. All I'm hearing is insult after insult. On both sides."

"There's nothing creative about insulting a whole group of people," Ms. Sterling went on. "Mollie, you say you've spoken with somebody about publishing this project. Is this really a project you want to put your name on?"

Mollie bit her lip and lowered her eyes. She didn't answer.

"I know I told you all that you should feel free to write whatever you want to write in this group, but I want you both to think about why it is you're writing what you're writing."

Tank knew exactly why he was writing what he was writing. To pass fifth grade!

"Is it because you really have something to say about the opposite sex? Or are you just trying to amuse your classmates? It seems to me you're both looking for ways to divide people when I think it would be more productive to look for ways to come together."

Yes, but males and females will never come

together, Tank thought. They're just too different.

"Well," Ms. Sterling said, pushing back her chair. "I think that's all the time we have for today."

Everyone else picked up their stuff and filed out of the room quietly.

"For what it's worth, I still think your book is funny," Travis said.

"Me too," Ned said.

Tank couldn't hear what the girls were saying to Mollie. But by the way they were patting her shoulder and glaring at Tank, he could guess.

Once everyone else had left, Tank and Mollie went to the Children's Room to get Gracie. When they got there, Tank could hardly believe his eyes.

Gracie was chasing some kid around the bins of baby books yelling, "Give it back! Give it back!"

The kid had Gracie's book bag. He must've thought he was really something, picking on a girl who was clearly a grade or two younger than he was.

"Uh-oh. Where's the librarian?" Mollie asked as Tank marched over to the little brat.

But Tank didn't care about the librarian.

"Hey," he said, grabbing the kid by the shirt. He wasn't much younger than Tank, but he was a lot smaller. Tank could take him.

"What do you think you're doing?" Tank asked.

The kid's smile turned to a look of horror. "N-nothing," he said, dropping Gracie's book bag.

Mollie grabbed it and handed it to Gracie.

Tank got right in the kid's face. "Are you picking on my stepsister?"

"N-no. We were just goofing around."

Tank tightened his grip on the kid's shirt. "You pick on my stepsister again, I'll break your face. Understand? In fact, if you so much as look at her funny, I will hunt you down and—"

"What is going on in here?" A librarian asked as she marched into the Children's Room. "There is no fighting in the library!"

Tank tried to explain that that other kid was picking on his stepsister.

"He's the same kid who was bothering me a couple weeks ago," Gracie said.

"There is no fighting in the library," the librarian repeated.

She didn't call their parents, but she did make all four of them leave. As soon as they were all outside, the other kid took off running.

"Yeah, you better run!" Tank called after him.

Gracie looked up at him with big, puppy-dog eyes. "Thanks, Tank," she said.

Mollie snorted. "Way to solve a problem, Tank."

"Hey, it's better than giving the kid the silent treatment!"

"Oh, yeah?" Mollie smiled. "We'll see what your mom has to say about that."

**\* \* \***

*why do girls ware so much make up?*

*Many people don't know this, but girls come from other planets. Its true. They are beemed here like in Star Track. They ware makeup to cover up their alien spots. So no one knows theyre really from other planets.*

*Why do girls wear make-up that sparkles?*

*Many girls ware makeup that sparkels. What is the deal with that? Well, the sparkel stuff is poison. It can kill you if you eat it. So if girls put that stuff on their faces then they know that no boy will ever want to kiss them.*

Why are girls afraid of spiders?

Many girls are afriad of spiders. Do you know why? Its because the avrage spider is smarter then the average girl. Spiders make silk, which is something most girls cannot do. They are also more bewtiful than girls. Have you ever seen a spider up close? Then you know Im telling the truth. Its scary for a girl to know that a spider is smarter and prettier than she is.

Why do girls give you the silent treatment when they're mat at you?

# 10
# It's Only a Little Punch

**W**hat do you mean you got kicked out of the library?" Mom asked. Mollie had pounced on Tank's mom the minute she got home from work.

"I wasn't fighting," Tank argued. "I was just talking to this kid who was picking on Gracie."

"That's right," Gracie spoke up.

Molly shrugged. "We still got kicked out because the librarian thought you were fighting," she said.

Man! Tank thought Mollie should've thanked him for defending her sister instead of ratting him out. That was a girl for you.

Mom listened quietly to the whole story, which Mollie, Gracie, and Tank all took turns telling.

Finally, Mom said, "It was nice of you to stick up for Gracie, Tank. But getting into a fight is not the way to solve your problems. We've talked about this. We've talked about this a lot."

"I know," Tank said. Frankly, he was tired of talking about it. Mom just didn't understand the way guys worked.

"This may have been the way Harry solved

problems, but—" Mom began. But Tank tuned out there. The guy had been gone for four years, yet Mom still blamed just about everything that went wrong in their family on Harry and his bad temper.

This had nothing to do with Harry. Maybe this wasn't the way Mom wanted Tank to solve problems, but she had to admit, it worked.

That night, after Tank finished going over his math with Dennis, he set his stuff in his room, then wandered around the house looking for Gracie. But she wasn't in the house at all. She was out in the backyard, swinging.

At first he just watched her from the kitchen window. He tried to remind himself that she was not his problem. Plus he had enough to worry about, what with trying to pass fifth grade, writing his book, being Jason's agent, dealing with Mollie, et cetera.

But Gracie was just a helpless little kid. She couldn't take care of herself. And well . . . Tank knew he could at least give her a few pointers. So he went outside, traipsed across the grass, and sat down on the swing beside her.

"Hey," he said, his swing swaying slightly back and forth.

"Hey," she replied, eyeing him curiously.

Except . . . Tank wasn't quite sure how to begin.

"Did you want something?" Gracie asked as her swing began to slow.

Tank twisted his swing around. "Well," he said. "I just . . ." How should he put this? "I just wanted to tell you you shouldn't let people push you around so much."

Gracie's swing was stopped now. She pushed her foot into the dirt. "I don't let people push me around," she said in a small voice. "They do it without my permission."

"Well, you shouldn't put up with it," Tank said. "You gotta act tough. If people think they can walk all over you, they will. Show them you're tough!"

Gracie wrinkled her nose. "But I'm not tough."

"Well, you have to act like you are. Otherwise you may as well be wearing a sign around your neck that says, 'I'm a wuss. Pick on me.' You gotta get rid of that sign and put on a new sign that says, 'Don't mess with me!'"

"How?"

"I'm glad you asked," Tank said. He hopped off his swing. "Come on. I'll show you."

Gracie's butt remained firmly attached to the swing. "Are you going to show me how to fight? I don't want to learn how to fight."

"I'm not going to show you how to fight. I'm going

**117**

to show you how to defend yourself." What was it with girls and fighting?

Gracie still wasn't getting off the swing, but at least Tank had her attention.

"Okay, step one," Tank said. "Body language. If you stand like this," Tank hunched his shoulders and dropped his head the way Gracie usually stood, "your body language says 'pick on me.' But if you stand like this," Tank lifted his shoulders, tightened his jaw, and narrowed his eyes at Gracie, who flinched in response, "your body language says 'don't mess with me.' Does that make sense?"

Gracie nodded slowly.

"Then why don't you come over here and try it?"

Gracie obediently slid off the swing and shuffled over to Tank.

"Okay, don't walk like that," Tank said. Man! This kid needed a complete overhaul. "You look like a scared little rabbit. Walk like this." Tank sort of stomped across the grass.

A small smile played at the corners of Gracie's mouth as she copied Tank's stomp.

"Again," Tank said. Stomp! Stomp! Stomp!

Gracie followed. Stomp! Stomp! Stomp!

"Better. Okay, now let's fix the rest of you. Head up, shoulders back. That's right!" Tank said when

Gracie sort of did what Tank was doing. "Except you need to put a scarier look on your face. Then look the other person in the eye, and while you're looking, I want you to think the words: 'I can take your head off if I want to!'"

"'I can take your head off if I want to,'" Gracie repeated. Then she looked up at Tank. "Except I'm not really going to do that, right?"

"Well, no. You're not going to take anyone's head off. But you have to look like you could. You have to look MEAN! Like this!" Tank barred his teeth and growled.

Gracie made a sound somewhere between a whimper and a growl.

"ARRRRR!" Tank growled.

"Arrr!" Gracie repeated.

"Make it scarier," Tank ordered. "Make your eyes and mouth look meaner when you do it."

Gracie clenched her teeth and made her eyes into angry little slits. She almost looked like she could do damage with those eyes.

"Yeah, that's good!" Tank nodded. "Okay, if someone is picking on you, all you have to do is make your face look really mad and say really loud, 'KNOCK IT OFF!'"

"Knock it off," Gracie said.

"No. KNOCK IT OFF!" Tank cried, stomping his foot.

Gracie jumped at the sound of Tank's voice. But then she squared her shoulders and tried again. "Knock it off!"

"Louder! KNOCK IT OFF!" Tank roared.

"KNOCK IT OFF!" Gracie roared back. This time there was fire in her eyes. And she was plenty loud.

In fact, she was so loud that Mom cranked open the window. "Are you two fighting out there?"

"No," Tank and Gracie said at the same time.

"Tank is playing with me," Gracie said with a smile.

Mom looked a little doubtful, but she cranked the window closed and stood watching the two of them.

"Make sure you're standing tough and say it just like that," Tank instructed. "For one thing, the kid will be thrown off guard. He won't know if you're going to rip his head off or not, but he'll stop and think about it. Plus, if you say it really loud, you'll probably get a grown-up's attention and they'll make him stop. It's like tattling without actually tattling."

"Oh," Gracie said, like she hadn't thought of that before.

Tank kept working with Gracie on how to walk, talk, and look tough until it got dark outside. She was getting better! Tank wouldn't exactly say he was afraid of her when they quit, but it was possible another seven-year-old would think twice about messing with her.

That night, Tank was lying on the bottom bunk staring at his *Guide to Girls* while Zack got ready for bed. He'd already written the header for his next page: *Why do girls think fighting is such a big deal?* He was trying to think of a really funny answer for that question, but then he got to really wondering about it.

Why wouldn't Gracie let him teach her how to fight? Why did Mollie write that stuff about boys thinking with their fists instead of their brains? Why did girls think fighting was so terrible?

"Hey, Zack," he said, tapping his pencil against the metal frame. "Did you ever wonder why boys fight, but girls don't?"

"What makes you think girls don't fight?" Zack asked. "They fight. I think they fight worse than boys do."

"Well, yeah. But it's different with girls. They don't *fight* fight. Not like boys."

"That's because girls don't like to get their hands dirty," Zack said. "If you ask me, girls fight nastier than boys do. With girls, it's all psychological."

"What do you mean?" Tank asked.

"Well, girls stop talking to you when they're mad at you. And they hold grudges. And they talk about you behind your back."

"True," Tank said. "Plus you have to watch your back if a girl is mad at you. You never know when she might try and get even."

"Exactly. Guys just don't think about stuff. You always know where you stand with other guys. But girls? Man, that can change practically every hour."

Zack flipped the light switch and climbed up to the top bunk. But Tank still had more to say.

"Don't you think the way boys fight is better than the way girls fight?" Tank asked. "I mean, sure we punch each other now and then. But it's only a little punch, and then it's over. What's the big deal?"

At first Zack didn't answer.

"Zack?" Tank peered up at the top bunk, wondering whether Zack had actually heard him.

But finally Zack answered. "The big deal is we usually punch first and think later."

That wasn't exactly what Tank had expected his brother to say.

"Remember Harry?" Zack asked suddenly.

That was the second time that day Harry had come up. "What about him?"

"Is that the kind of guy you want to be when you grow up?" Zack asked. "The kind of guy who hits his wife and kids?"

"I'm not going to be that kind of guy," Tank said.

"How do you know?"

"I just know."

Tank heard Zack flop around on the bed above him then, like he was rolling over. And then he heard even breathing. Tank assumed Zack was asleep.

But then, just as Tank was drifting off to sleep himself, Zack whispered, "Do you want to know the real reason Dagmar broke up with me?"

Tank opened one eye. "Okay."

"She broke up with me because I punched a hole in her wall."

# 11
# The Mistress of Evil Butts In

Tank almost cracked his head when he sat up. "You punched a hole in Dagmar's wall? You mean her bedroom wall?"

"Yup."

"With your hand?"

"Yup."

Whoa! Tank reached for the light switch.

"Don't turn on that light," Zack growled from the bunk above Tank.

"Okay," Tank said, his hand frozen in mid-air. Slowly, he shifted to a more comfortable sitting position. "So, when did this happen? When did you put a hole in her wall?"

"The day we broke up."

Tank had been to Jason's house several times since then. Why didn't Jason ever mention the fact that Zack had put a hole in his sister's wall?

Tank tried to remember what had happened that day. That was the day he and Mom and Dennis had met with those people at school and signed that summer school contract. Zack had come home that night all bummed out. And then he got mad at Tank.

"You said you didn't know why Dagmar dumped you."

"Well, it was so unexpected. She just said she didn't like to be around me when I was mad. This was totally out of the blue. She said I scared her. Then she said she thought we should take a break from each other. I got kind of mad, and I punched her wall, and the wall sort of caved in there. Then she freaked out, and she told me to leave, and she said she never wanted to see me again."

"Whoa," Tank said. He didn't know what else to say.

"I guess I really did scare her," Zack said.

"D-do Mom and Dennis know about the hole?" Tank asked.

"No."

Maybe Jason and his parents didn't know, either. Maybe Dagmar never told anyone what happened to her wall?

"Remember when Harry left and Mom made us go for counseling?" Zack asked.

"Yeah."

"I think maybe I should go again. Because I don't want to hit people or scare people. I don't want to put holes in walls. And you shouldn't be hitting people, either, Tank. Like Mom always says, there are other ways to solve problems."

"Okay," Tank said. He didn't quite believe it, but Zack had certainly given him something to think about.

"Have you talked to Dagmar at all since you broke up?" Tank asked.

"Nope."

"Do you think you ever will?"

"I don't know. I don't know what to say to her."

"You could say, 'sorry I put a hole in your wall,' and then tell her you'll fix it."

"Maybe," Zack said. "I'll think about it."

* * *

The next time Tank was over at Jason's house, he was dying to get into Dagmar's room and see the hole for himself. But he didn't know how to do it without telling Jason why he wanted to get in there.

The two of them were sitting at Jason's computer playing video games. It was kind of boring, really. Jason was shooting spaceships and Tank was sitting next to Jason, supposedly offering moral support. But really he was rehashing everything Zack had told him the other night. He just couldn't believe his brother had punched a hole in someone's wall.

"So, is Dagmar here?" Tank asked casually.

"No. She's at the pool with her friends," Jason replied, still shooting. "Why?"

"No reason," Tank said. He stood up. "I need to use the bathroom."

"Okay," Jason said.

Tank closed Jason's door on his way out. Luckily Dagmar's door was open. He quickly stepped inside and peered around, looking for the hole.

It took a while to find it. But there it was on the other side of the door. A fist-sized indentation.

Tank laid his hand into the indentation. *What was wrong with Zack?*

Of course, Zack hadn't actually hit *Dagmar*. He'd just punched her wall. He had hit Tank on occasion, though. And Tank had hit back. But neither of them had ever actually hurt the other.

Would either of them ever really hurt someone? Tank didn't think so. He didn't like people messing with him. And he wasn't above scaring someone who was messing with him, but he'd never actually hurt anyone. Would he?

What about that kid who was picking on Gracie? If the librarian hadn't shown up, would Tank have hurt that kid? Tank was pretty mad. He wanted to make that kid quit picking on Gracie.

Was Mollie right? *Did* boys think with their fists rather than their brains?

No. Maybe some boys did. But not Tank.

Tank wouldn't have hurt that kid at the library. He just wanted to scare the kid into leaving Gracie alone. Nothing wrong with that. Was there?

Tank went back to Jason's room. Jason had quit their game, and he was swiveling back and forth on his desk chair, waiting for Tank. He had a pretty serious look on his face.

"Listen, Tank," he said. "We need to talk."

Tank's heart thumped. "Okay," he said nervously. Was this about Dagmar? Did Jason know about the hole in her wall, after all? Was he going to say he didn't want to be friends with someone whose brother would put a hole in his sister's wall?

Jason motioned for Tank to sit down on Jason's bed. So Tank did. Jason took a deep breath, but no words came out.

"What?" Tank asked. If it was something bad, he wished Jason would just spit it out.

Jason took another breath. "I'm getting a little tired of *The Dagmablob,*" he said finally.

"What do you mean you're getting tired of *The Dagmablob?*" What did that mean?

Jason picked up The Dagmablob Returns from his desk and stared at the red cover. "I think it's because nothing new is happening. Kelly says it's just the same old thing. The Dagmablob just keeps attacking, destroying or sliming things—"

"Wait a minute!" Tank leaped to his feet. "When did the *Mistress of Evil* read your movie script?" Jason had never read it at the writer's club.

Jason bit his lip. "She stopped by once or twice."

Once or *twice?* Tank started pacing back and forth. He knew she'd come over to Jason's house once. Had there been another time, too? What was she doing hanging around all the time?

Tank combed his hands through his hair. "And now you think your movie script isn't any good? Because *the Mistress* says it's not?" Who did she think she was messing with Jason's mind like this?

Jason shrugged. "She's right. It isn't very good. We started talking about another story idea instead—"

"You what?" Tank interrupted. This was getting to be too much. Tank had to sit down.

"We've been talking. She's got a video camera. So she was thinking we should get together and make a movie."

"You and her?"

"Me and her and lots of people," Jason said. "You,

too! It takes lots of people to make a movie, you know. First we have to write the script. Then we have to find people to act in it. Then we have to film it and edit it. What do you think, Tank? Wouldn't it be fun to actually make a movie rather than just write a movie script?"

Tank had to admit it sounded fun. Really fun. Except that it was the Mistress of Evil's idea rather than his or Jason's! But still . . . "We might have better luck selling *The Dagmablob* to Hollywood if we had an actual movie to send rather than just a movie script," Tank admitted.

"That's right!" Jason said. "But," he paused. "The thing is . . . Kelly doesn't really like alien movies all that much."

That figured. "So, just because she doesn't like alien movies we have to do something else?" Tank asked.

"Well, I kind of want to do something else, too," Jason said.

"Like what?" Tank asked. What could possibly be better than *The Dagmablob?*

"Well, Kelly and I were thinking maybe a murder mystery."

"Hmm." Tank liked murder mysteries. He liked alien movies better. But murder could be fun.

Especially if the Mistress was the one who got murdered.

"Have you started a new script?" Tank asked.

"Not yet, but I've got some ideas. Do you want to see?"

"I guess." It didn't hurt to look at other ideas.

Jason opened his notebook to the first page, which was now a list of murder mystery ideas rather than the beginning of *The Dagmablob Returns*. Tank also noticed there were bits of paper stuck in the spiral edge.

"What happened to *The Dagmablob Returns?*" Tank asked.

"Oh, I tore those pages out and threw them away," Jason said.

Tank gasped. "You threw them away! How could you throw them away?" What kind of writer throws away his own work?

"I told you, they weren't very good."

"I thought they were good."

"You're the only one who did," Jason said. "It's no big deal. Here, tell me which of these ideas you like best." He shoved the notebook onto Tank's lap.

Number one was about a group of people who are invited to a house for dinner and one by one the guests start to disappear.

"I think I've already seen that movie," Tank said, pointing to number one.

"Yeah, I know," Jason said. "That was Kelly's idea."

"Big surprise," Tank muttered.

Idea number two was about a teacher who gets murdered. That sounded okay. Number three was about a blind girl who overhears a murder and then has to find the murderer before he finds her.

"Oh, please," Tank said. "I suppose number three was the Mistress of Evil's idea, too?"

Jason winced. "Yes. And don't call her the Mistress of Evil."

"Why not?"

"Because she doesn't like it."

"So what?" It was a good name. And it fit her.

"I'm serious, Tank. If you keep bugging her . . . " Jason broke off.

Tank frowned. "If I keep bugging her, what?"

"If you keep bugging her . . . sh-she might not let you work on the movie."

"What? I'm your agent! She can't stop me from working on it." Tank would love to see her try.

"Well, she's the one with the video camera," Jason pointed out. "So yeah, she can stop you."

Tank didn't like the sound of that. What was Jason saying? That in a war between him and the

Mistress of Evil, the Mistress would win?

"I really want to make movies, Tank," Jason tried to explain.

"I know," Tank said. "So do I."

"No!" Jason shook his head. "You don't understand. I *really* want to make movies. I want that to be my job when I grow up. It's what I've always wanted to do. So if you mess this up for me by making Kelly mad—" Jason didn't finish his threat.

"Okay, okay!" Tank held up his hands. "I promise I won't say or do anything to upset the—to upset *Kelly*. Okay? I'll even pretend she's not evil, if that's what you want." Though that would be a stretch.

Jason smiled. "Good. Now, a bunch of us are getting together Friday morning to go over ideas for the script—"

"Did you say Friday morning?" Tank asked. He couldn't do it then. He had his math class.

"Yeah. Mollie said that was a good time for you guys."

"Mollie's part of this, too?" Tank moaned.

"Yeah. She and Kelly are friends. And she lives with you, so I thought—"

"Well, you thought wrong," Tank interrupted. "I can't do it in the morning. We'll have to change it to Friday afternoon."

"Mollie said you guys can't do it afternoons," Jason said. "She said her sister or your brother could watch Gracie in the morning, but you don't have anyone to watch her in the afternoon."

"We don't need anyone to watch her. We can bring her along. Maybe we'll want a little kid in the movie."

"Well, I have to go to my grandma's on Friday afternoon," Jason said. "What do you have to do Friday morning? Why can't you come then?"

Tank did not want Jason to know what he was doing. "I just can't," he said. "And Mollie knows I can't!" This was just another way for her to get back at Tank for Dennis making her take down her web site.

"But why can't you?" Jason insisted.

"Because I can't!" Why was Jason being such a pain?

"Well, fine. Don't tell me then," Jason said.

"I won't."

Jason's shoulders drooped. "I thought we were friends, Tank."

"We are friends."

"Then why won't you tell me?"

"Why do you have to know?"

"Because everyone else can make it Friday morning. If we have to find another time, I want to at least know why."

"Well, I'm not going to tell you why!" Tank yelled.

"Then I'm not going to change the time!"

"Fine!"

"Fine!"

Man! Tank thought. When had Jason grown a backbone?

# 12
# The Mistress, Murder, and Mayhem

Tank's mind was not on math on Friday morning. It was on Jason, and the Mistress, and Mollie, and murder mysteries. In fact, a murder plot was starting to come together in Tank's head.

*How could Jason even think about making a movie without Tank?*

"Come on, Tank. Concentrate!" Mr. Grisham said. "I know you can do these problems."

"How do you know?" Tank muttered.

"Because you just did them last week."

"That doesn't mean I can still do them this week."

Mr. Grisham sighed. "Just stop and think about what you're doing." He slid the book closer to Tank. "What's the first step?"

Tank glanced down at the book. He had a feeling that "decide on a murder weapon" wasn't exactly the answer Mr. Grisham had in mind.

"What do we have to do to the denominators before we can add the numerators?" Mr. Grisham asked.

Tank thought for a minute. "Make them the

same?" he guessed.

Mr. Grisham nodded.

Tank worked the problem. Eventually he came up with 11/12 for the answer.

"That's right," Mr. Grisham said. "See? I told you you could do it."

"Sure," Tank said. But he wasn't getting too excited yet.

"Should we try another practice test?" Mr. Grisham asked.

"If you want," Tank said. Even though he could do these problems with Mr. Grisham and with Dennis, he still screwed up on the practice tests.

"Just take your time," Mr. Grisham said as he handed the paper to Tank. "Think through all the steps. And then don't forget to check your work."

Tank took a deep breath, then got to work. He had the rest of the period to do the practice test.

He tried to take his time. He tried to think through all the steps. It wasn't his fault his mind kept wandering.

He wondered how many people had shown up to work on Jason's movie? Who all had he and the Mistress of Evil invited? Had they invited any other boys, or was it all girls? Were they coming up with good ideas?

Before Tank knew it, twenty-five minutes had passed.

"Are you finished, Tank?" Mr. Grisham asked.

Tank looked down at his sheet. He still had two problems to go.

"That's okay," Mr. Grisham said. "Let's see how you did on the problems you did."

With red pen in hand, Mr. Grisham went over Tank's test. Tank groaned with every check mark Mr. Grisham made. Tank ended up with four points out of twelve.

"I'm never going to get this, am I?" Tank said as he wadded up the test.

"Now, wait a minute." Mr. Grisham grabbed Tank's arm. "Don't do that. I want you to take that home and figure out what you did wrong on each of those problems. That'll be your homework for tonight."

What was the point? Tank wondered. "I'm going to flunk summer school, aren't I, Mr. G.?" he said.

Mr. Grisham sat back in his chair. "If that's your attitude, yes, you probably will."

"Hey, it has nothing to do with my attitude," Tank said. "I'm busting my butt here. I show up every single morning, even when I have better things to do. I do all the assignments. I turn them in. But I still can't pass the tests. How am I going to pass fifth-grade math if I can't pass the tests?"

"I don't know, Tank," Mr. Grisham said. "But I'll tell you this. Success is a choice. People who expect to succeed usually succeed. And people who expect to fail, usually fail."

This was supposed to make Tank feel better?

Mr. Grisham took the wadded-up paper out of Tank's hand, smoothed it out, then handed it back to him. "Now, I want you to go home and redo the problems you got wrong. Then I want you to come back here tomorrow with a positive attitude—"

Tank opened his mouth to argue, but Mr. Grisham cut him off. "Positive attitude," he repeated. "I guarantee you will never fail at anything you go into with a positive attitude."

How could Mr. Grisham guarantee something like that, Tank wondered.

When Tank got home, Zack was in their room, packing a bunch of stuff into a brown paper bag.

"What have you got there?" Tank asked.

"None of your business," Zack said.

Like Tank really cared. He tossed his backpack onto the bottom bunk and decided to go get some lunch.

"Wait a minute," Zack called him back.

"What?"

Zack went over to Tank and showed him what was in the bag. "It's putty. For fixing Dagmar's wall."

"You're going to fix her wall?"

"Yeah. I'm going to try and talk to her, too. You want to come with me?"

"You want me to come with you to talk to Dagmar?" Tank asked. It wasn't like he and Zack were friends or anything. They were brothers; that was all.

Zack shrugged. "You can hang with Jason. I figure she's less likely to kick me out if you're there to see her brother."

"Yeah, the only problem with that is I'm not sure Jason and I are actually speaking right now."

"I thought girls were the ones who stopped speaking," Zack said. "Boys just punch each other and then they're done. Isn't that what you said?"

"Yeah, but I don't really want to punch Jason."

"Good," Zack said. "That's good."

"Jason and me will figure things out. Just not right now."

"Okay," Zack said, folding the top of his bag back up. "Wish me luck."

"Good luck," Tank said.

\* \* \*

"I heard you and a bunch of people got together this morning to talk about our movie. Mine and Jason's," Tank said when he, Mollie, and Gracie sat down to lunch.

No one else was home.

"First of all," Mollie said, her mouth full of peanut-butter-and-banana sandwich. "It's not your and Jason's movie. It's everyone's movie. Everyone who's working on it. And second of all, it's too bad you couldn't be there. We had lots of fun." She smiled.

"You know what I did this morning, Tank?" Gracie asked as she bit into her peanut-butter sandwich.

Tank didn't really care what Gracie did this morning.

"You got Jason to set it up for this morning just to bug me," Tank said, ignoring Gracie.

"Oh. And you didn't tell your Mom and Dennis about my web site to bug me?"

"I watched *The Karate Kid* this morning," Gracie said to no one. Because no one was listening to her.

"I didn't tell my mom and Dennis anything," Tank said. "My sister did. I didn't even know there was anything wrong with your web site until my sister told me."

*Man, would she ever give that a rest?*

"We are still not even for that, Tank," Mollie said,

**141**

sliding her chair back and taking her half-eaten lunch to the sink.

"Oh, come on!" Tank said. "So you had to take your web site down. Big deal."

"It *is* a big deal," Mollie said. "And it's not just because I had to take the site down that I'm mad."

"Then why are you mad?"

"You figure it out," Mollie said as she left the room.

Tank threw his hands up in the air in frustration. He may have been writing a book about girls, but he had to admit it. He knew nothing about them. Absolutely nothing.

"Now can I tell you about *The Karate Kid?*" Gracie asked once Mollie was gone.

Tank stared at Gracie. "I've already seen *The Karate Kid*. You don't have to tell me about it."

"Oh," Gracie said. "That's good. Then you know what I mean when I say I'm kind of like Daniel and you're kind of like Mr. Miyagi."

"The old guy with the chopsticks? How am I like him?"

"Because he taught Daniel how to defend himself against bullies just like you're teaching me how to defend myself against bullies."

Whoa! Tank didn't quite know what to say to that. Mr. Miyagi was like the coolest character in the whole movie.

"Can we practice again today?" Gracie asked.

"Yeah, I guess." How could Tank refuse?

So after lunch Tank and Gracie went outside. Tank could tell she'd been working on her walk and her look. She looked even tougher now than she did a week ago.

"I changed my mind about the punching," Gracie said. "I want you to teach me how to punch."

"I don't know, Gracie." Tank hesitated. Was teaching her how to punch somebody really such a great idea?

"Why not? You said all I have to do is punch somebody once and they'll never bother me again."

"Yeah, I know, but—" But when Tank thought about Zack, and his old stepfather, Harry, he just wasn't sure anymore that teaching Gracie how to fight was the right thing to do. She wasn't a fighter. Why turn her into one?

"Just keep working on how you walk and how you talk, okay? If you look like you're someone people shouldn't mess with, they won't mess with you."

"Okay," Gracie said, confused.

"Listen, I should go in," Tank said. "I've got some stuff to do."

Since he was already acting like this really great

person, maybe he'd see if he could tackle the math on his own. Before Dennis looked at it.

But when Tank got to his room, he discovered his backpack was missing.

# 13
# This Is War!

Tank stormed across the hall and tried the door. It was *his* room, after all. But the door was locked. Big surprise.

"WHERE'S MY BACKPACK?" Tank pounded on the door. He could hear the radio, so he knew Mollie was in there. It had to be Mollie because Gracie was outside.

"WHERE'S MY BACKPACK?" he yelled again.

Finally, the door opened. "I don't know what you're talking about," Mollie said. But Tank could tell by the little half-smile on her face that Mollie knew exactly what he was talking about.

"This isn't funny," Tank said, trying to calm his racing heart. "I need that backpack." His math stuff was in there—his homework, his math book, and his calculator. So was his *Guide to Girls*.

Mollie shrugged. "Then I hope you find it."

"You know where it is!"

"Do I?"

"Yes. You do."

"Sorry," Mollie said, closing the door.

Tank tried to push it back open, but he was too

slow. Mollie got the door closed and locked.

Well, Tank could open a locked door now. He went back into his and Zack's room, got his pin and came back. He wiggled the pin back and forth in the hole, but for some reason the door wasn't popping open this time.

"That only works when someone isn't pushing the lock in," Mollie informed Tank from the other side of the door.

Tank kicked at the door in frustration. Who did she think she was digging into his backpack and stealing his stuff?

"You won't get away with this," Tank warned.

No response.

Tank was not a tattletale, but he didn't know what else to do. *He needed that backpack!* So as soon as Dennis got home that night, Tank ran to the kitchen. "Mollie took my backpack," he said.

"What?" Dennis was reading the mail, so he probably only listened with half an ear.

"It had my math in it. And my writing book. So I haven't been able to do any schoolwork today."

Now Tank had Dennis's attention. Dennis frowned. "Mollie!" he called. "Mollie, can you come here, please?"

Tank heard the bedroom door creak open, then

Mollie came out acting like nothing was wrong. "What?" she said.

"Honey, Tank says you took his backpack," Dennis said. "Did you?"

"No."

"You did, too!" Tank argued.

"I did not! You can check my room if you don't believe me," Mollie told her dad.

They all trooped back to Tank's old room. It about killed him to see that all his Sci-Fi movie posters had been replaced by posters of kittens. Dennis searched under the bottom bunk, behind the door, under the desk, and in the closet.

"It doesn't look like it's here, Tank," Dennis said.

"Told you," Mollie said, her arms folded across her chest.

"Are you sure you didn't just forget where you left it?" Dennis asked Tank.

"No! Mollie took it. I know she took it! She practically admitted it earlier."

"I did not!" Mollie said. She turned to her dad, her eyes brimming with tears. "He's just saying that to get me in trouble. He hates me. He hates all of us. He doesn't want us to be here."

Tank didn't want them here. But what did that have to do with anything?

"I'm sure that's not true," Dennis said, wrapping his arms around Mollie. "I know Tank likes having you here as much as I do." Tank tried not to snort. "Why don't you try and calm down. Then we'll see if we can help Tank find his backpack."

So Tank, Dennis, and Gracie searched the front of the house while Mollie searched the back. About two minutes into the search, Mollie called out, "I found your backpack, Tank." She brought it to him in the family room. "It was under your bed."

"It couldn't have been!" Tank said. For one thing, there was too much other junk under there. It never would have fit.

"That's where I found it," Mollie said with a shrug.

"Well, the important thing is you got it back, Tank," Dennis said. "Now, if you don't mind, I think I'll go start dinner. Your mom will be home soon and I'd like to have dinner ready when she gets here."

Tank watched Dennis walk away. Dennis just couldn't accept the fact that his own daughter was a *thief!*

"You really should take better care of your things, Tank," Mollie said as she turned and headed down the hall.

"Uh-huh," Tank said. He unzipped the backpack and peered inside just to make sure everything was there. All his math stuff was there. But . . . Uh-oh. *Where was it?*

Tank rifled through every item in his backpack. It was no use. His *Guide to Girls* was gone!

"Hey!" Tank immediately took off after Mollie. This time he managed to catch her before she escaped into her room. "I need my notebook, too."

"I don't have your notebook," she replied.

"Come on," Tank said. "I need it. It's for school."

"For school? Right!" She started to go into her room, but Tank grabbed her arm.

"It is!"

Mollie scowled. "Let go of me!"

"Then give me my notebook!"

"I don't have it."

"I'm not goofing around here. I need that note-book. If I don't get it back, I don't pass fifth grade!"

Mollie grinned. "Yeah, I saw that summer-school contract in the front pocket of your backpack. You really are flunking fifth grade. What kind of a moron flunks fifth grade?"

Tank tightened his grip on Mollie's arm. He wanted to hurt her. He wanted to hurt her, bad. "If you say anything about that to anybody—" Tank hissed.

"What?" Mollie asked, getting right in his face. "What will you do, Tank? Will you *hit* me?"

Tank let go of Mollie's arm then. Because just for a second there, he thought he really might hit her. He could feel the blood pulsing through his veins. His whole body trembled.

"Just give me back that notebook," he said through gritted teeth.

But Mollie just went into her room and slammed the door.

* * *

On Saturday night, Dennis grilled hamburgers and hot dogs for dinner. After dinner, Tank went back out to the grill to roast marshmallows. While Tank stood over the warm grill with his skewer, something at the very edge of the grill caught his eye. It looked like a scrap of burned-up paper. But the scrap wasn't completely burned. There was writing on it. That wasn't *Tank's* writing, was it?

It was too hot inside the grill to dig the scrap out with his fingers. So Tank popped the half-roasted marshmallow into his mouth, then poked the scrap with his skewer. He could read three words on the scrap: *Why Do Girls.*

*It was a page from Tank's notebook!*

Oh, Mollie was going to get it now. Tank stormed

back into the house. His mom and Dennis were cleaning up the kitchen. Gracie and Mollie were playing a computer game in the family room.

"Look at this!" Tank cried, shoving his skewer toward his mom.

"Tank, be careful!" Dennis said.

"Do you know what this is?" Tank shouted. "This is a page from my book! The book I have to write to pass fifth grade. I found it all burned up in the grill."

"How did it get there?" Mom asked.

"One guess," Tank said, shooting death looks at Mollie in the family room.

"You think Mollie did this?" Dennis asked.

"Did what?" Mollie glanced up from the computer like she had no idea what they were talking about.

"BURNED MY BOOK!"

"You burned Tank's book?" Mom asked.

Mollie gasped. "I didn't know that was Tank's book," she said all innocent.

Sure, she didn't!

Mollie stood up and walked into the kitchen. "Remember, I said I needed a notebook?" she asked Mom. "I showed you that blue one and asked if I could tear out all the pages that had writing on them and you said I could."

Tank whirled to face his mother. "YOU SAID SHE

COULD TEAR PAGES OUT OF MY BOOK?" he screeched.

"I said you could tear them out," Mom said, ignoring Tank. "I didn't say anything about starting a fire and burning them in the grill."

"But—that was my book!" Tank cried. How could Mom have given Mollie permission to tear pages out of Tank's notebook?

"You can't possibly think that starting a fire by yourself is an okay thing to do," Dennis told Mollie. "Don't you know how dangerous that is?"

Mollie's eyes filled with tears.

"You could have hurt yourself. You could have hurt someone else. You could have burned the whole house down," Dennis went on.

"What about my book?" Tank stomped his foot. Didn't anyone care about his book? The book that he needed to write if he wanted to pass fifth grade.

"I'm sorry, Tank," Mom said. "I didn't know that was your book when Mollie came to me."

"No, but she knew it," Tank said, pointing at Mollie. "She stole it out of my backpack and—"

"I did not," Mollie cried. "I found it. In the family room."

"LIAR!"

"I did!" Mollie insisted as she grabbed onto

Dennis's arm. She was crying openly now. "Daddy, you have to believe me. I didn't know it was his. Really, I didn't."

Dennis didn't actually believe her, did he?

"Well, whether you knew the notebook was his or not, I think you owe Tank an apology," Dennis said.

Mollie turned her tear-stained face to Tank. "Sorry," she said in a voice that Mom and Dennis probably thought was sincere. But Tank knew better.

"Apology *not* accepted," Tank said, glaring at Mollie. Then he turned to his mom. "What am I supposed to do now? I had a lot of pages written on. It's not fair that I should have to start over."

"We'll talk to Mr. Burns," Mom replied. "We'll tell him what happened."

"If you keep writing a page a day, I'm sure he'll understand," Dennis said.

And that was the end of it. Mollie didn't get grounded or lose privileges or anything. It wasn't fair. If Tank had taken Mollie's book and burned it in the grill . . . he shuddered. He didn't want to think about what would've happened if the whole situation had been reversed.

**\* \* \***

Monday afternoon was just as hot and sticky as all the other days Tank, Mollie, and Gracie had walked to the library. But at least today they didn't have the sun beating down on them, too. Dark storm clouds were gathering in the west.

"Slow down, you guys!" Gracie panted. "You're walking too fast!"

Tank knew Gracie was running to keep up. He wasn't trying to get so far ahead of her. It was Mollie he wanted to keep ahead of. He was so mad at her that he just couldn't deal with her.

"Yeah, Tank," Mollie called. "Slow down."

Tank just kept moving. He pretended Mollie wasn't there.

"What's the matter, Tank. Are you not *speaking* to me?" Mollie taunted. "I thought you said boys don't give people the silent treatment."

Do not respond, Tank told himself. Do not respond.

They got to the library just as the first rumbles of thunder sounded.

Tank and Mollie walked Gracie back to the Children's Room, but Gracie stopped just outside it. "I don't want to go in there today," she said.

"Why not?" Mollie asked.

Gracie got up on her tiptoes and whispered,

"That boy's in there again."

Tank looked. Sure enough. That same kid who had taken her backpack last week was standing in front of one of the computer catalogs."

"Just ignore him," Mollie said impatiently. "If you ignore him, he'll ignore you."

"And if that doesn't help, just remember what I taught you," Tank told Gracie. "Stand your ground. Don't let him mess with you."

"Oh, Kelly's here," Mollie said, glancing over her shoulder. "I have to go. See you after class, Gracie." And then with a wave of her hand, she was gone.

Why was Mollie in such a hurry? Tank wondered. She wasn't going to go tell the Mistress about him flunking fifth grade, was she?

"I don't want to go in there," Gracie said again, pulling on Tank's arm. "Please don't make me go in there."

Tank did not have time for this. He had to get to the writing club and see what Mollie was up to.

"Just go in there, okay?" Tank said impatiently. "You'll be fine. Mollie and I will be back in an hour."

Gracie hung her head. Tank felt a little like a jerk. But what else was he supposed to do? If Gracie's own sister wasn't hanging around, why should he? He turned around and headed back to Meeting Room B.

Jason was waiting for him outside the room. When Jason saw Tank coming, he walked toward Tank. "I need to talk to you," he said.

Tank figured Jason wanted to make up after their fight. Which was fine. But Jason had something else on his mind. He leaned close to Tank and said in a low voice, "Do you know what those girls in there are saying? They're saying you flunked fifth grade."

Great.

"That's not true, is it, Tank?"

Tank took two steps toward the meeting room, then stopped. It just never ended with Mollie. Why did she hate him so? What did he ever do to her to deserve all this?

"Tank?" Jason said.

Tank had to get out of there. He had to get out of there *now*.

# 14
# Making Peace

**W**ait up, Tank!" Jason called. But Tank kept right on running. There was a clap of thunder and then the rain started. It poured down in sheets almost right away, soaking Tank to the skin. But he didn't care. He darted across the street, splashing right through the puddles. Not that he could avoid them. The street was quickly turning into one big puddle.

"TANK!" Jason yelled behind him.

*Why didn't Jason just go back to the library?*

"Come on, Tank! Wait up!"

Tank glanced over his shoulder. Jason was gaining on him. Where did Jason learn to run like that? Tank was dying here. He didn't know how much longer he could run.

"LET'S GO OVER TO THE PICNIC TABLES," Jason shouted, waving toward the covered shelter at the park they were passing.

Oh, what the heck, Tank thought. He was tired of getting rained on. And it didn't look like Jason was going to give up. So he veered over to the park, splashing through the soggy grass. He didn't stop until he was under the shelter. Then he collapsed onto one of the picnic table seats.

Jason plopped down on the seat across from him. Chests heaving, they lay down and listened to the rain pounding the metal roof above them.

Once they both caught their breath, Jason sat up. "Why didn't you tell me you flunked fifth grade?"

"I haven't officially flunked yet," Tank said, staring up at the ceiling. There was a wasp's nest in one corner.

"What do you mean you haven't officially flunked yet?"

"I won't know for sure until the end of the summer whether I flunked or not."

Jason waited for Tank to go on.

Tank took a deep breath, then let it out. He might as well tell it all. "See, there are all these things I have to do," he explained. "First, I've got this math tutor. He's Mrs. Grisham's husband. You know, Mrs. Grisham from school? I have to see him every weekday morning. That's why I couldn't get together Friday morning."

"Ah," Jason said.

"That's not all." Tank sat up and faced Jason. "I also have to do all this writing. That's why I started my *Guide to Girls*. The deal was if I did better in math and filled a notebook with writing over the summer, I could still pass fifth grade."

But Tank wasn't doing so great in math. And he didn't even have his *Guide to Girls* anymore. Who was Tank kidding? He didn't have a prayer. He was going to be back in Mr. Burns's fifth grade class again next year while Jason and everyone else went on to middle school.

"So, why didn't you tell me?" Jason asked.

Tank shrugged. "I didn't want you to think I was stupid."

"I don't think you're stupid. Everybody's good at different things, Tank. You're maybe not great at school. But you're fun to hang out with, and you've got good movie ideas, and you're a good agent."

Tank snorted. "I'm just a kid. I'm not really a good agent."

"I think you are. You're the one who figured out how to send a movie script to a real Hollywood producer. You're the one who keeps sending it out even though we keep getting rejection letters."

"That's because I know it'll sell eventually," Tank said.

"That's what makes you such a good agent. You believe in us. You believe we're really going to sell our stuff to Hollywood."

Tank looked down at his feet. "We are unless I flunk fifth grade."

"What does flunking fifth grade have to do with us

selling a movie script to Hollywood? Do you think they really care about fifth grade in Hollywood?"

Tank hadn't really thought about it. It was Jason that he cared about. Would Jason want an agent who flunked fifth grade? Even more important, would he want a *friend* who flunked fifth grade? A friend who was still in elementary school?

The rain was slowing down. It still poured down the roof of the shelter, but if Tank looked out into the park, he could see that the lines of rain had grown much finer. The worst of the storm was over.

"I guess I can understand why you were afraid to tell me," Jason said after a little while. "There's something I'm a little nervous about telling you, too."

Tank looked at Jason. "What?"

"You know Kelly?" Jason said carefully.

"Yeah?" *The Mistress of Evil.*

"I . . . kind of like hanging out with her."

Tank curled his lip. "What do you mean you like hanging out with her?"

"Well . . . she's kind of cute, don't you think?"

Tank just about choked. "Cute?" Puppies were cute. Kittens were cute. The Mistress of Evil was definitely not *cute.*

"Come on, Tank. Don't you think she's a little cute?"

"Not really." Tank wrinkled his nose.

"Well, then," Jason said, sitting up a little straighter. "You must need glasses."

"No, you're just weird," Tank replied.

Jason grinned. He glanced out across the park. "Hey, it looks like it stopped raining. Maybe we should head back to the library?" He glanced down at his watch. "The writing club is almost over."

Tank wasn't sure he wanted to go back to the library. Everyone there knew he was flunking fifth grade. It was just a matter of time before the whole world found out.

"Maybe I'll just go on home," Tank said. "Could you tell Mollie and Gracie that I went home?"

"I think you should come back to the library," Jason said. "If you don't, everyone will know that what Mollie said really got to you."

Jason had a point there. *Act tough*. That was what he'd told Gracie. Except, what good would being tough do him now? It wasn't going to help him pass fifth grade.

Whether he flunked or not, he was going to have to find a way to deal with those kids and the teasing that was sure to come. Preferably without bopping anyone.

A light breeze rippled through the trees, sprinkling

water on Tank and Jason as they headed back to the library. But it didn't matter since both boys were already soaked.

When they turned onto the street the library was on, Tank saw most of the writing group milling around outside. What were they doing? Waiting for Tank and Jason?

As soon as Mollie noticed Tank and Jason, she came barreling down the street toward them. Tank's spine stiffened. Just the person Tank *didn't* want to see.

"There you are!" Mollie cried. "Do you know where Gracie is?"

Huh?

"She isn't with you?" Mollie looked on either side of Tank, and behind him, as though he were hiding Gracie.

"No—"

"The children's librarian said Gracie hasn't been in all day." There was real alarm in Mollie's voice. "Are you sure Gracie went in there? Did you actually see her go in?"

"Did you?" Tank asked. But he already knew the answer to that question. Mollie had been in such a hurry to go blabbing about Tank to her friends that she hadn't even stuck around to make sure her own sister was okay.

Not that Tank had been any better. He'd been in a pretty big hurry to find out what Mollie was going to do. Neither one of them had actually seen Gracie go into the Children's Room.

"Great," Molly said, crossing her arms. "Nobody knows where she is. And she's been missing a whole hour."

"Well, she's got to be around here somewhere," Tank said, glancing around. How far could a seven-year-old old get all by herself?

"Don't worry, you guys," the Mistress said, taking charge. "We'll find her. We'll all help you look for her."

Before Tank knew it, the Mistress had divided everyone into groups of two and pointed out where they should look. One group headed over to the park. Another group headed up First Street. A third group headed the opposite direction on First Street. And Jason and the Mistress went back inside the library to see if they'd somehow missed her.

That left Tank and Mollie standing alone outside.

"I can't believe you just left her there," Mollie said.

"Hey, you left her, too," Tank pointed out. "And she's *your* sister, not mine." Your responsibility, not mine, he thought.

"Yeah, well, Dennis is *my* dad, but that doesn't

stop you from worming your way in with him!"

Tank blinked. "What are you talking about?"

"I'm talking about my dad! You act like he's just as much your dad as he is my dad."

Tank's mouth fell open. "I do not!"

"You do, too. You guys are always doing stuff together in his office at night."

"Math stuff," Tank pointed out. It wasn't like they were doing anything fun.

Mollie turned away. "I don't care what you're doing. Besides, we should be looking for Gracie, not arguing."

"Yeah, we should," Tank agreed.

They started walking around outside the library, their feet growing wetter with every step. They checked the picnic tables; they checked the outdoor story area, and they checked behind every bush and shrub around the library. No Gracie.

All the while they were searching, Tank thought about what Mollie said about him and Dennis. It sounded like she was *jealous*. Jealous of him?

How could that be? Mollie had everything going for her. She was smart. It sounded like she had a lot of friends. And she had a pretty cool dad. But she only got to see him in the summer. Tank saw him every single day. Even when Mollie was here, there were still days when Tank saw more of Dennis than she did.

That explained a few things.

"So, is that why you're always so mean to me?" Tank asked as they started toward the parking lot. "Because you're mad that I get to see your dad all the time and you don't?"

"The only reason I'm mean to you is because you're mean to me," Mollie said, refusing to look at him.

Tank stopped walking. "I was maybe a little mean last year," he admitted. He was mean to lots of people last year. And the year before. But he was a different person then. He didn't have many friends. He didn't have Jason. Plus his mom and Dennis had just gotten married, and he didn't know how that was going to go.

But . . . maybe Mollie was just as unsure about all of that family stuff as he was? She sure wasn't any nicer of a person than he was. And she certainly didn't understand boys any better than he understood girls.

Whoa. Was it possible that deep down, he and Mollie weren't really so different? Tank didn't want to think about it.

"Listen, I'll make a deal with you," Tank said. "You be nice to me, and I'll be nice to you. We'll call a truce, okay?" It wasn't much, but it was a start.

Molly thought about it for a couple of seconds. Surprisingly enough, she said, "Okay."

While they were shaking hands, Jason came running out of the library. "Tank! Tank!" he called. "Phone call for you."

Uh-oh.

Tank and Mollie dashed into the library. The person at the front desk held a phone out to him. "Are you Tank?"

"Yes," Tank said, taking the phone. "Hello?"

"Tank?" It was Zack. "Did you know Gracie walked all the way home by herself?"

"She walked all the way home? In the rain?" Tank was impressed.

"Gracie's home?" Mollie mouthed at Tank. Tank nodded.

"I don't think she walked in the rain," Zack said. "She's not wet or anything. She was just sitting on the front porch when I got home from work. She said she couldn't get in because she didn't have a key. Why did she walk home by herself, Tank?"

"Uh . . . " Tank glanced at Molly. They were both to blame for this one. "What did she tell you?"

"Nothing. She just said, 'Because I felt like it.'"

"Mollie and I will talk to her when we get there,"

Tank said. Then he hung up.

When Tank and Mollie got home, they found Gracie on the swing set out back.

"What were you thinking?" Mollie stormed right over to Gracie. "You can't go running off like that. Nobody knew where you were."

"I knew where I was," Gracie said with a shrug. Her swing swayed slightly from side to side.

"Yeah, but we didn't," Tank said.

"So? You guys don't care about me."

"What are you talking about?" Mollie asked.

"We care," Tank said. He was surprised to discover there was a part of him that really *did* care. Gracie had become . . . like a sister to him. How had *that* happened?

"If you really cared, you wouldn't have made me go into the Children's Room all by myself when that boy was in there," Gracie said.

Tank and Mollie glanced at each other.

Mollie knelt down on the grass in front of Gracie. "Gracie, you can't be afraid to go in the Children's Room just because that kid is there."

"That's right," Tank said.

"You need to find a way to deal with him," Mollie said.

"I don't know how to deal with him," Gracie said,

digging her toe in the dirt.

Tank threw up his hands. "I've been showing you what to do for the last few weeks."

"You've been teaching Gracie how to fight?" Mollie asked Tank.

"No. I've been teaching her to stand up for herself. That's not the same as fighting." Tank used to think it was the same. Now he thought there had to be ways to stand up for yourself without fighting. Ways to stand up for yourself without being mean to other people.

Mollie pressed her lips together. "Well," she said to Gracie. "Whatever you do, you can't go running off like you did today."

"Yeah," Tank put in. "Because no matter what you think, we really were worried."

"O-*kay*," Gracie said. "Next time I'll find another way."

\* \* \*

On Monday, Tank and Mollie actually walked Gracie into the Children's Room before they went to the writing group. All three of them were relieved to see that the boy who'd been giving her such a hard time wasn't there that day.

Gracie went right over to the dollhouse.

"She'll be okay," Tank said as he and Mollie left.

Tank was relieved that nobody in the writing club asked him whether he was really going to flunk fifth grade. He didn't want to talk about that.

People did ask him about his *Guide to Girls,* though. Mollie had told everyone the previous week that she had destroyed his book.

"Did you start another *Guide to Girls?*" Travis asked.

"No," Tank said. He'd been writing a page of *something* every day. Usually just some rambling on his life. His mom had said she'd talk to Mr. Burns about what happened to his other notebook. So hopefully if he just kept up the writing, it would be good enough.

But he didn't have the heart to start another *Guide to Girls.* Writing a book wasn't like doing math. You couldn't just start over. If you lost it, it was gone.

Besides, what did Tank *really* know about girls, anyway? What did anyone know? They were like an alien race that no one ever really understood.

"I think you should start another one," Ned said.

"So do I," Travis said.

"Do you know what I think?" the Mistress of Evil asked from across the table.

Tank wasn't sure he wanted to know, but Jason spoke up right away. "What do you think?"

She grinned at Jason, then turned to Tank. "I think we should all work on a book called *The Boys and Girls Guide to Each Other*. Except it'll be different than your and Mollie's books. For this book, the boys will write about boys and the girls will write about girls. You can tell us what you want to know about girls and we'll tell you what we want to know about boys. And that's what we'll write."

"What an interesting idea," Ms. Sterling said.

"I like it," Mollie said.

"So do I," Jason said.

"Do you think we could get it published?" Katie or Caity asked as she tapped her pencil.

"I don't know," Mollie said. "Publishers don't like to publish books by kids."

"But I thought you were getting your other book published," Alex said.

"I thought I was, too," Mollie said glumly. "But my mom's agent didn't know I was serious. When she found out I really had a book, she said she was sorry, but she couldn't take work from children."

"The same thing happened to us with our movie script," Jason said. "A couple of the movie producers we sent it to said they don't take work from children, either."

Tank snorted. "Like just because a kid did it, it

couldn't possibly be good."

"Well, if you keep up your writing, I have no doubt you'll all be published authors one day," Ms. Sterling said.

"And published movie makers," Tank added.

"Hey, I've got an idea," Kelly said. "Maybe when we finish our *Boys and Girls Guide to Each Other*, we can turn it into a movie. Like a documentary. We could do everything ourselves. Film, cast, edit. What do you think?" She was looking right at Tank.

Tank had to admit it was a good idea.

"But, first we need to do our murder mystery," Jason said. "Which reminds me, we need to find another time to work on that. Tank can't come in the mornings."

"How about Tuesday and Thursday afternoons?" Brandi suggested.

Mollie glanced at Tank. "We'll have to bring our little sister."

*Our* little sister? Tank thought. But he kind of liked how that sounded. Gracie was his little sister. His and Mollie's.

"That's okay," Jason said. "She can be in the movie, too."

When class was over, Tank and Mollie went back to the Children's Room to get Gracie. She was reading at the table right by the door, so she saw them coming before they ever got to the Children's Room.

She jumped up and ran to meet them. "Guess what?" she said, hopping up and down.

"What?" Tank and Mollie said at the same time.

"That kid came in here again."

Tank and Mollie glanced at each other. This was *good* news?

"I did what you told me, Tank. I stood up straight and tall—I'm almost as tall as he is—and I put on my don't-mess-with-me look, and . . . he didn't mess with me!"

"I told you," Tank said.

"He just looked at me, then walked away."

"At least you didn't get in a fist fight," Mollie said. "When Tank said he was teaching you to stand up for yourself, I was sure he was teaching you how to fight."

"Hey," Tank said, insulted. "I'll have you know it's been one hundred and two days since my last real fist fight!"

Mollie raised an eyebrow. "You're turning over a new leaf?"

Tank shrugged. "Maybe." There were worse things that could happen.

# 15
# What I Learned on My Summer Vacation

*Dear Mr. Burns, Mrs. Meed and everyone else who gets to deside weather I pass fifth grade or not,*

*You talked to my mom about my book, right? You know I started a book called* Tank Talbott's Gide to Girls. *Then my stepsister burned it. Girls!*

*But Ive been doing lots of other writing. And I joined a writing club at the libbary. In fact, you can even ask Ms. Sterling about my book if you dont beelieve I realy wrote one. She heard parts of it.*

*So here is everything I wrote this summer. Well . . . everything except the stuff that got burned. I hope its good enuff.*

*—Tank*

## What I learned about Fighting:

*Peeple say fighting isn't the answer. That there are better ways to solve problems. The thing about fighting is its quick. And if your good at winning fights, people wont mess with you. Because they wont want to fight you.*

*But you have to ask yourself wether you're the kind of person who wants to solv problums with your fists. Because you might never get a girlfrend or have kids if your one of those peeple. I don't want a girlfrend now but I might want one somtime.*

*Also peeple like you better if you don't fight peeple all the time. Take it from me. I know.*

## What I Learned about Familys.

*There are lots of diffrent ways to make a famly. A family can be peeple who are reelated. Or it can be peeple who live together. Or it can be other stuff. My sister Lauren doesn't live with us, but she's still famly. Dennis isn't reelated to me, but he and my mom got marred so he lives with us. He's a pretty good guy to have in your famly. Except he has three kids and theyre all girls!*

*Anna is okay becaus shes older and I hardly ever see her.*

*Gracie isn't to bad eather. She's only 7 so she hasnt groan into a real girl yet. Also she likes cartoon network.*

*Mollie's my age. We fight alot. But its getting better.*

*Anna, Gracie and Mollie aren't my faverite peeple, but I'm getting used to them. In fact I even get mad when people aren't nice to them. And I worry about them if theyre not were their sposed to be. And I think I'm even going to miss them when thay go back to florida.*

*There are lots of diffrent ways to become a famly but I think most of the time it just sort of happins by axsident. That's the way it happend with me and Anna and Gracie and Mollie.*

what I learned about being a agent:

*Being a agent is alot of work. Espeshally if you're the only one who beleives in your clients work.*

*Sometimes even your client quits thinking his work is good. But an agent never gives up. Just like a friend.*

What I Learned about Freinds:

*Jason Pfeiffer is a really good guy to have as a frend. I dint want him to know I was flunking 5th grade because I was afraid he wouldn't like me anymore. But guess what? He found out. And he din't even care.*

What I learned about girls:

*Girls are very unusal creechures. I thought I understud them, but I don't. Maybe I never will?*

# CENTRAL ELEMENTARY SCHOOL
## DISTRICT 97, JOHNSON COUNTY

### ACADEMIC PROGRESS REPORT

NAME:

*Thomas Talbott*

E = EXCELLENT
S = SATISFACTORY
N = NEEDS IMPROVEMENT
U = UNSATISFACTORY (FAIL)
I = INCOMPLETE

| | FINAL GRADE |
|---|---|
| Mathematics | S |
| Reading | S |
| Writing | S+ |
| Spelling | N |
| Social Studies | S |
| Science | S |
| Art | E |
| Music | S |
| Physical Education | S |
| Conduct | S- |

PASS TO __6th__ GRADE:

RECOMMENDED ___✓___

NOT RECOMMENDED _____

X_____
PARENT SIGNATURE

**Dori Hillestad Butler** is the author of several books, including the novels *Alexandra Hopewell, Labor Coach; Sliding into Home; Do You Know the Monkey Man?*; and another book about Tank and Jason, *Trading Places with Tank Talbott*. Dori and her family live in Coralville, Iowa. You can visit her web site at www.kidswriter.com.